—

After the Fall

the

Fall

and Other Stories

After the Fall

and Other Stories

ZHOU TAI AN

PARTRIDGE

To order additional copies of this book, contact
Toll Free 800 101 2657 (Singapore)
Toll Free 1 800 81 7340 (Malaysia)
orders.singapore@partridgepublishing.com

www.partridgepublishing.com/singapore

Contents

After the Fall

SHE'S HAPPY TO see me again today, and for that I am glad. Sometimes the toxins in her system pain her so much she can't sleep, and sometimes she can't even get out of bed or speak properly. But today she greets me with a smile and I return the gesture.

We sit down and begin talking. I ask all my routine questions. How are you? Does it hurt especially bad anywhere? What have you been doing lately? Is the medicine working? Slowly we come to the last one, the all-important one, but also the one that I both dread and desperately want to know the answer to.

Do you ever feel like flying again?

It is the whole point of the program. The federated government would not otherwise spend billions on rehabilitation, doctors, medical examinations and everything that they are currently doing. The more poetically inclined among us might term it a form of atonement, but the concerted efforts of the doctors have a more practical concern. Angels, with their reinforced bone structure, greater adaptability and of course, ability to fly, would be of great use in the colonization efforts.

But for me all that exists in that moment is her, and the answer that I both seek and back away from. No, that's not entirely correct. I am aware of my eyes flickering over the medical report, the distant hum of the generator, the soft glow of the lights in the room. On some level, at least. All my attention is focused on her though. The way she shakes her head. The play of light on the sheen of her hair, the slightest move of her head, the flicker of her eyelids.

It's a dance we both go through every day. I ask the same questions and she gives the same answers. Eventually when we get to the end, she tells me what I most fervently wish to not hear, I accept it with what grace I can muster, and I leave and go back to the seemingly endless rounds of scans and analyses and reports which all tell me the same thing - that have been telling me the same thing for the last 2 months.

There is nothing physically wrong with her. In fact, she is among as healthy a sample (I cringe mentally as I use that word) as we have ever found. Whatever toxins that remained from the bioweapons have been purged by her system a long time ago. Others are not so lucky. In the adjoining building are those that still suffer from residual mutations, who were near ground zero when the bombs struck later in the war. I hear horror stories from the other doctors, whispered consultations about who is going to live and die.

The war may have ended some time ago, but Earth's resources are not infinite. In fact, they are anything but. Triage is still a reality now, but instead of being for our troops, now we are deciding which of our former oppressors will survive. Humans, deciding the fate of those who had so long been the judge of ours. The irony does not escape me.

But maybe the ones who are mutated are in fact the lucky ones. There are cures for them, simple, straightforward -if painful and expensive. We know what to do with them. The chemical structures for the mutations and diseases, though complicated, can be understood in time. The Exceln supercomptuer, so adept at coordinating bombing runs and frontal assaults, provided equally effective at decoding the mysteries of angel DNA.

All this doesn't help me, though. Why won't she fly? Why won't she even attempt to? I run through all this in my head, argument and counterargument, knowing that it is likely to be useless. She might not be even able to tell me if she knows. Medical science has advanced so much, but it is next to useless against whatever malady she has. I find myself turning back to authors at the turn of the millennium, who helped cure patients with only the most primitive knowledge of quantum brainwaves and neurointervention. They had little to work with, and yet they managed to work miracles with only the most primitive of instruments.I have sore need of their abilities now - where our nanomachines have tried and failed, perhaps their methods and ways, old though they are, might yet prevail.

Days pass, and I bury myself in books and microfilms, searching desperately for answers to questions that were never meant to be asked. Glimmers of hope appear from time to time, but I often feel like a blind man in a dark cave, unable to grasp even the slightest hint of something that might help.

My investigations do bear fruit after some time, and I learn new ways of healing. Apparently simple conversation is the key to unlock the secrets of the mind and soul. Let the patient speak, the books counsel, and they will eventually tell you all that you need to know. Patience is the watchword - I see that phrase repeated time and time again, but time is something that is in short supply.

It all seems too easy. I am just to speak to her, and that will somehow aid in her cure? But I am at my wit's end, and having tried everything, all that remains is the impossible.

★★★★★★

I enter her room as I always do, to find her sitting at the window, as she always is.

I'm not sure what I should say to her. In fact I am never sure what I should say to her...but I guess that might actually be the point. If the doctors were certain of what treatment would work, she would be flying by now.

I begin with the most simple of statements. I am mindful of everything that I have read so far...the books advocate going as slow as possible. When there is no sickness of the body, it must be something that resides in the mind, and that is always the most delicate of matters.

"How do you feel?" I am taught that that should be the opening statement. It invites a response, and is open-ended enough that the patient will not feel unduly pressured.

"Alright, I guess." She sighs and one wing droops and trails listlessly on the spotless floor. I don't reply that she looks anything BUT alright. That is not the recommended course of action. We are supposed to let the patients speak for themselves and not interpret what they say...reflection, not response.

Moments pass and she does not do much else besides look from side to side. Finally, I venture another question.

"How are you doing these days?" I judge it to be a neutral enough query, but it does not have its intended effect. All she does is sigh again, close her eyes and then look at the ground. I wait a few minutes more, but she does not say a thing.

We are getting nowhere. I curse my superiors for pushing her so hard - they think I do not know how they maintain constant surveillance of her through remote cameras hidden in her room, but I do. She has precious little privacy, and not enough room to heal. The treatment of invisible wounds is not something that can be managed by amateurs, and their clumsy meddling threatened to undo what little good I have accomplished so far.

I take a deep breath and try again. My anger, no matter how justified, will not help here. I school myself to be non-judgmental, and continuing asking questions in what I hope is a measured tone of voice. Is the food to her liking? How about rest - is she sleeping well? Would she like to go outside, or read a book? All simple, non-threatening inquiries. Anything to get her to reply, to open those eyes hooded in pain and mouth shut in silence.

Nothing. After three more questions or so I fight to keep from sighing and leave the room slowly and quietly. There is nothing to be done right now - if she will not talk, she will not. Waiting is hard indeed when the rewards are so dearly anticipated, but all the texts that I have read counsel patience, and so I try and stifle my mounting frustration. If she is to be cured at all, in will not be in the space of a single night. And if today was a failure - and I have no way of knowing if it was or not - then there is always tomorrow.

★★★★★★

I try taking breaks here and there, not coming every day but on alternate days, and it seems to help somewhat. She looks at me when I come through the door now. Her wings, though still non-functional, do not trail along the ground anymore. A little color has come back to her cheeks...not a lot, but enough to gladden me.

I think we are getting somewhere, but I cannot be sure. She seems to even enjoy my visits now - she smiles sometimes, and answers my questions once in a while. But we are still not one step closer to getting her to fly. My joy at these small (but not insignificant) developments is overshadowed by my worry about her well-being. She still doesn't look healthy - her hair lies lank and still on her head, and she moves slowly, too slowly. At times she moves from bed to chair and almost trips, and I have to rush to her side to make sure she does not fall.

Despite all this, the pressure from my superiors is mounting. They want to know what is wrong, and fast. If we can cure her, then maybe we can cure others, and if we can cure others... I tell them not to rush, that this is not something we can hurry. It is the science of the mind that we are dealing with here, and that has no quick fixes or answers, no matter how much they may want them.

But for all my words and placations I am worried as well. What if she doesn't respond to the treatment? What shall I do then? I check the books and they say to simply give the patient more time, but that is also a resource that is in finite supply. I would like to pretend that we have forever, but we most certainly do not. If we wait too long, then there is the very real chance that the higher-ups will withdraw my funding and support, and maybe even take her away to another facility. They are sure to push her far too hard there, and who knows what much happen? I have heard the horror stories from the other researchers -

It will do no good to worry overmuch. I close my eyes, sigh and open the door that leads to her room. Today is another day, and with each day comes hope - hope for the future, hope for healing, for myself and her. At least, that is what I keep telling myself.

She smiles when she sees me, which I take to be a good sign.

"How are you feeling today?" I ask the same question each day. Some routine would do her good.

"Better, thank you." And it does look like it. There is a sheen in her silver-grey hair that wasn't there before, and a lightness to her face that makes me feel much better than it really should. I try to cultivate an air of detachment but I cannot quite contain my joy at the change in her. It's working...all this talking is really working!

We chat a while about this and that, what books she is reading - last week she timidly asked for a few, and I had them sent up to her rooms as quickly as possible. She likes picture books, especially those about nature. She tells me about the trees I marvel that how simple conversation could have wreaked such a great change in her. The ancients obviously knew what they were talking about. In a time without advanced science, they had somehow managed to uncover secrets of the mind and soul that still proven relevant to this day. How much bloodshed and strife would we prevent if we had just talked to each other...but that is my researcher's mind wandering again.

Our conversation goes in circles for a while. I want to simply ask directly if she thinks she might be up to flying, but something tells me that that might be too much, too soon. So instead I keep to the same safe topics. What has she done today? Is the food to her liking? Tell me about the stories you are reading in the books.

That last question seemed to spark in her, and I let my own cares and worries float away for a while as I listen to her chatter animatedly about the giants and trolls and pixies that have tickled her fancy. It is a welcome distraction from us both, and for a short while we are able to take a much-needed escape from reality. Such is her enthusiasm that even I am drawn into it, forgetting the need for objectivity and end up

She grows tired after about an hour of talking, and I draw things to a close as adroitly as I am able. I think we are making progress. At the very least she is talking now, and from there perhaps more healing can come.

★★★★★★

I've suggested painting as a means to recovery. They call it art therapy, and it is supposed to work wonders and reach places that mere words cannot. I am skeptical but remain hopeful - everything the books have said has been right so far.

She seems to take it to well enough. I've ordered paints sent to her room, along with the picture books that she seems to like so much. Tales of fantasy are forgotten in favor of pastel colors and bright shades. Though the images in the books are all of woodland scenes, with trees and green grass aplenty, she does not paint any of those. Instead, she favors pictures of the sun, the clouds, and the open sky. The symbolism is not lost on me - she desires freedom, and all we do is keep her in a locked cage.

Would that it were within my power to grant her that which she wishes. But she cannot have freedom unless she learns to fly once again - and if she does, then wouldn't see already be free? The problem and the solution are one and the same. It is a strange dance that we are engaged in, a game of getting her to do what she already wants to do, but cannot.

I watch her paint via remote camera. It would be too intrusive to actually be in the room itself with her – I consult once more with the sages of old, and they say that my presence might be construed as being too aggressive. The last thing I want to do is jeopardize the gains that we have both so painstakingly made, and so I judge that checking on her progress remotely is probably the best course of action.

She paints slowly, deliberately, drawing each line with infinite care and control. She sketches the outline of a circle, then daubs at it ever so gently with yellow that she has mixed before, her brow creased in concentration. And with those simple motions a sun is born. Next she streaks white across the already snowy canvas and there are clouds.

I find myself lost in the delicacy and simplicity of her craft. More than once I think that all I would ever desire is to be there, watching her at work. I forgot to take notes or observe anything, and I feel renewed gratefulness for the computer monitoring software whose readouts will let me at least pretend that I am working when they are checked later.

I wonder what she is thinking as she sketches each golden orb and fills in each ivory wisp of cloud. Does she miss the past? Does she remember the times when her brothers and sisters rained destruction down on our cities from on high? I often think of asking her about the war, but I think that would be even worse than asking whether or not she is ready to fly. If she does remember, it may be far too traumatic for her to even attempt to recall. And if she doesn't, there is no point in dredging up what should be forgotten.

We have to look to the future, and not the past...but what if the answers we seek may lie in places we once thought were dead and gone? It is a conundrum that resists my best efforts to unravel.

★★★★★★

The other scientists are hounding me to produce results. Work on the orbital station is proceeding apace, and they need new workers desperately...almost as desperately as I want to be cured. I explain to them that we are at a delicate stage in her treatment and that I cannot risk jeopardizing what progress we have already established, but my pleas fall on deaf ears. They only care about one thing – getting her to fly. It is the same thing I care about, but our ways of going about it are completely different.

I worry myself if I have grown too close to her. The books say that we cannot risk becoming too enmeshed with our charges, lest that impair our judgment. But in my case I think it has already happened.

I want her to be able to fly with a desire that surprises even myself. It's not just about the recolonization efforts, or the validation of my theories. I do not care for career advancement or academic success or any of those things that my cohorts seem to obsessed with. I have grown to realize that I am striving for something far greater. I just want something to brighten her wan face, to lend light to her eyes. To make her dreary imprisonment just that little bit more palatable, so that every day that she wakes she has something to look forwards to. To make her happy.

I want to help. I can even believe that I am helping. She speaks more at each session now, and I think the pictures are a step in the right direction – she has begun to speak, albeit haltingly, about what she wants to do when she is well enough to leave the medical facilities. I struggle to keep my composure and not become too excited, for fear of triggering a negative reaction in her. There is a lightness in a step that wasn't there before, and sometimes when a brief quiet space falls into the flow of our conversations, she casts shadowed eyes to the ceiling and even seems to remember what happened to her so many years before.

We are getting somewhere. I believe that...I have to believe that. The time we have both spent together is forging a bond between us - something powerful and precious which will in time transcend the fears and sorrow of the past. Or at least, that is what I keep on telling myself.

★★★★★★

One day out of the blue, she suggests taking a walk around the gardens. I am only too happy to accede to her request, though I am also careful to make sure that our paths do not take us too close to any of the internment camps that are perilously close to where we are walking. I don't think it would do her good to look on our other prisoners. She may suspect the truth - wounded or no, she is no fool - but I do not want to take any chances.

It is a beautiful day. The sky is clear and unmarked, the trees and green and vibrant, and even the very air smells fresh and new. She seems invigorated by the physical activity and she chatters to me endlessly about what pictures she is painting and what books she is reading. As we turn the corner of one of the paths wending their way through the fields we stroll through, she almost skips and dances.

I am seized by a sudden desire to take her hand, but I beat it back down with all the self-control I can muster. Not only would it be too much, too much, it would be completely and totally inappropriate. I am here to help her regain flight not, not...not whatever else it is I want to do. I shake my head and simply follow her as she makes her meandering way through the greenery around us.

She stops suddenly and points to the sky. I follow her outstretched finger's motion, but I cannot see what means. Sensing my question, she asks one of her own.

"What is out there?"

"What do you mean?" I am confused, but I hope I don't let it show.

"Beyond the sky. One of the nurses said it was space...what is that? Is that another sky? Past the sun and moon and clouds?"

I somehow sense that this is not the time to explain astrology to her. Nor can tell the truth behind her simply inquiries - that past that cloudless expanse of blue is the orbital space station that we need her assistance with. I simply smile and nod. Another sky...that is one way to put it. Black where this is blue, full of stars instead of clouds.

She falls suddenly quiet again, and I lead her back to her quarters.

★★★★★★

Weeks past, and I can delay things no longer. The time to try actual flight has come. I try to make it slow and painless as I possibly can, ensuring that no one disturbs us during our preparations, and telling the nurses to take extra-special care of her in the days leading up to our experiment.

I do not bother consulting the books. They have brought me to this place, but I doubt they have any more advice to offer at this point. This will be something only she and I can do.

I debate with myself endlessly about how best to go about actually getting her into the air. My mind suggests to me a myriad of options that I discard summarily - rocket-assisted flight, drugs to stimulate nerve endings, or even cybernetics. In the end I settle on the most simple of solutions. I will bring her to the gardens that seemed to so invigorate her, and let her try her best. Her wings which were had once lost their colors have regained some of their former sheen, and I take this to be a good sign.

It is a bright and cloudless day when we resolve to make out first attempt. I hold her hand as we walk out from her rooms, and I marvel at how small it seems in mine. I can feel her trembling and she makes no attempt to hide it. She is afraid, as I am. What if we fail? But on the other hand...what if we succeed?

We reach a small hillock and I nod to her. She nods back, closing her eyes in concentration. I let go of her hand and she walks forwards.

She takes one faltering step, and then another. I wait with bated breath, hoping against hope. Her wings flap once, and then again. I am struck by how delicate they look in the morning sun, their pristine whiteness making them appear almost transparent. I want to rush out, to reach out to her, clasp her shoulders and hug her to me, but I cannot. Fail or succeed, this is something that she must do herself.

The expression on her face pains me to even see it. What memories are rushing through her mind at this moment? I know from the doctor's reports that the nerves on her wings have been damaged, but they are still intact enough to let her feel physical pain. And I need no books or medical experts to know that the body and mind are linked, and when one hurts, so does the other. But I force all those thoughts from my mind and return to the moment, to the here and now.

Another step, another wing flap. Her steps come more easily now, beating a soft rhythm on the flat grass. Her pinions come down once, twice and it looks for one moment that she might make it. Time stops and my world contracts to the motion of her wings, the color of her eyes, and the sudden gust of wind that springs up.

But the very next second pain transfixes her face, and she stumbles. What should have been a step becomes instead a sudden lunge forwards, and she lists to the side, panting. Before I know it she has crumpled to the ground. I rush forwards to catch her, but I am too late. I cradle her gently in my arms, the notion of flight all but forgotten.

I wipe away the tears from her face as best as I am able. However painful the fall must have been, it does not compare to the anguish she must be feeling inside. She buries her face in my chest and I stroke her back with utmost care. Moments pass as we embrace, and I wish, not for the first time, that I could shoulder burden instead.

It is a slow walk back to her room. She leans on me the entire way there, barely able to put one foot in front of another. I lift her into her bed slowly and pull the covers over her. She falls asleep almost immediately, but it is a restless, fitful slumber. I watch her from my seat at the table as she twists and turns, moaning softly.

This is a setback that we will not easily recover from, but... but...we still have to try.

★★★★★★

I dread going to see her after what has happened. She hasn't spoken a word since then, and the nurses tell me that all she does is staring at the ceiling from dawn to dusk. After filing the relevant reports, I steel my nerves and make the short trip to her rooms.

It is worse than I feared. She sits on her chair, unseeing, and I feel that like all the work we have done was wasted. She is back to where she was before I commenced her treatment... no, even worse this time. At least then she looked at me when I spoke to her, and occasionally replied.

Now I have been sitting here for half an hour and all she has been doing is sighing. I fight back the irritation that threatens to overcome me. What she needs is patience, and time...the former which is in short supply and the latter which I have little of.

After what seemed like an eternity of waiting I venture a question. "How do you feel?"

She doesn't reply, instead looking at me with an expression bothering on disdain. Of course. She must feel terrible. Still, it had to be asked.

I fumble enough for something else to say. What could possibly get through to her in the state that she is in? Talking of books and pictures seems so paltry in the light of what she must have experienced. I want to ask her how I can help, but I she already knows that I wish to do so. Asking about her condition would just be too premature. But I must say something. I must get through to get somehow.

After a minute or so of deliberation I decide to take the plunge. "What is the matter?" There, I said it. It's out in the open now.

"Nothing." Another wingtip droops and her eyes avoid mine.

"You know that's not true." The words slip out of my mouth before I can stop them. I think it has gotten to me – the stress, the constant questioning from above, the sleepless nights spent poring over words and papers. Not to mention the fact that her failure weighs on me – if not as heavily as it does on her – a great deal as well. I am no angel, only human, and my frustration has apparently finally spilled over.

She looks at me almost angrily. I am happy to see the spark of emotion from her, but upset at her reaction. All my carefully cultivated detachment vanishes in that instant. I'm only trying to help...only trying to help! How can she not see that? What can else can I possibly do?

Our eyes meet and I feel the futility of the situation once again. What else can I say? We have reached a point beyond what the books have taught, what I myself can do.

Her eyes flash and she makes a sudden motion towards the door. She wants me to leave? Fine. I'll do that. Better than sitting here and wasting my time. I get up angrily and within minutes I am on my way back to my room. I regret my rash and impulsive movements even before I am halfway there. What kind of healer leaves his charge suffering all alone? What kind of scientist forsakes logic for anger? But in those moments everything seems too much to bear, and I want to do is bury my head in a book and shut out the world.

★★★★★★

I spend the next few days hiding from everything and everyone, swimming in what seems to be an endless sea of reports. I have work to do, I tell myself. Things need my attention. And on top of that, my behavior was unacceptable, thoroughly, completely and utterly unprofessional. I feel a need to redeem myself, to work hard enough that I can erase the memories of my outburst and failure both.

But deep inside I know that I am just avoiding having to see her. The expression on her haunts me...anger and bitterness is a potent mixture that cuts deep into my heart. I wonder for a moment who is hurting more at the moment – she or I.

I shouldn't have lashed out like that. I should have been more calm, more at ease. Steadier, more accepting. I turn back to the books once more, but all they say is that caretakers themselves need rest and relaxation. That is all well and good, but they have never had to deal with the fate of a race resting on the healing of a single girl before.

My emotions cool after a while and reason returns to me, along with other feelings...regret for harsh words spoken, and determination to see things through till the end. I cannot abandon her now, not in what may be her darkest hour. She is my charge and in my care, and books or no books, I will lead her into the sky.

I am not so blind as to see where this is leading. I have abandoned all pretense of keeping a safe distance from my patient emotionally, and I am entangled in her healing to may be considered an unhealthy level...but so be it. Science has not proven to have worked so far, and hotter emotions may prevail where rationale falters.

Or so I tell myself. In truth, all I want to do is see her smile again.

★★★★★★

We are sitting and talking again, and her disposition has improved considerably. She smiles more, and makes conversation, and is able to walk short walks in the gardens again. There has been no mention of books or pictures, but that is well enough. Some weeks have passed, and time has healed the sting of bitter failure somewhat.

Neither of us has apologized, but we didn't need to. When I had screwed the courage to appear in her room again, she greeted me the same way she always did. We fell to talking, and for once I am able to relax in her presence and put away the constant questions and examinations that I am seemingly forever engaged in. I allow myself to be grateful that she has not seemed to suffer lasting harm, and to take simple joy in her company.

As I sit in my chair, she reaches out a soft hand to take mine. I am not supposed to touch my patient, but there are so many things that I am not supposed to do that I have done that this is just one other forbidden fruit out of many. I return her smile with one of my own.

I think I am falling in love with her. I think I already have.

But as for her healing...there is not much else I can do at this point. I have tried everything I can, and all that remains is to... to what? A last consultation with the books reveals that there are things that even the ancients did not know. Maybe all I have to do is trust that mysterious entity know as fate.

I look down at our hands and I realize that without my knowing I have entwined mine in hers. I lift my head and meet her gaze, and I reach an outstretched hand to her to...to do what? What is it that I desire? What might bring us to the point that we both wish to be at, somewhere that is beyond this room and chairs in it. The sky is waiting for us, along with something more.

She averts her eyes, a faint blush coloring her pale cheeks, and I drop my hand embarrassedly to my side. We sit for a few moments longer and I think of what to say, but to my amazement I come up with nothing. Or maybe there is really nothing else that can be said.

★★★★★★

I think she is ready now.

The past month has been more of the same. The higher-ups hound me for reports, useless data continued to stream in, and I continue my daily visits to her. There been a slow and gradual shift in her that gladdens my heart to see. I was so worried that her failure would have scarred her beyond her ability to recover, but she has rallied gamely.

I judge that our bond has deepened till the extent that I do not need to fear rejection, and I am right. One day I ask her outright about how it felt to try and fail to fly. She looks at me straight in the eyes, blinks, and after a few moments begins to tell me.

It starts off slowly, with her pausing between each word and the next. She told me that her head started hurting first, but she tried to shut away the sensations and concentrate on walking instead. But the dull throbbing in her temples wouldn't go away, until, until...her recollections become more and more vivid the more she speaks.

She brings her knees up and clasps her arms around them, rocking back and forth in quick, sharp motions. This is obviously difficult for her, but I am patient. More than that I am somehow able to restrain myself from going over to embrace her. The most I will allow myself to do is place a hand on her shoulder as she reaches a particularly difficult place in her story. It seems to help, and she comes back to herself once more. She speaks until the flood of words grows from a trickle into a torrent and it is like she cannot stop herself even if she wanted to.

She remembered. She remembered everything before her fall. While the war was raging Dark, roiling. She was flying with her and a stray laser blast from the cannon emplacements tore through one wing - and then she remembers falling...an eternity of falling. The memories were so twined that to feel one was to feel the other...to fly was to fall.

As her story continues to unfold, I am not surprised to see tears trace their way down her cheeks, but I watch silently. All this seems to be helping though. Perhaps the books were right after all. The simple telling of one's story does heal in ways that cannot easily be seen.

It is a breakthrough, and I am. The next day - and in fact the week after - she is brighter and more cheerful than I have ever seen. She has taken to sketching again, and this time green grass and blue skies are once again her subjects. I am heartened by her recovery, and suddenly all the reports that I have to fill and people to answer with seem so insignificant in the face of this joy.

★★★★★★

Emboldened by our success, one day I throw caution to the wind and ask her directly if she wishes to fly.

She looks back at me with eyes brighter than I have ever seen and nods. I am reminded of a long-ago night when as a child, I looked up into the night sky and gazed in wonder at the twinkling lights above. This war before the wars, and the skies were still clear and dark when the sun went down. But what shines in her jet-black orbs now is more brilliant that the radiance I saw so many years ago.

The time has come, it seems. Once again, I do not bother with medicine or any other kinds of panaceas. I can sense her will and her intention, and those are what will bear her aloft. It is time to put books and cures behind us and trust in our bonds instead. Once again she takes my hand in hers and in her tiny grip I can feel the pulse of something greater than either of us.

We walk out to a grassy field - one of the few that has survived the devastation of the war. It is a cold, moonless night when we make our second attempt, and unlike the first I do not think of either good fortune or bad. After all this time I feel a kind of acceptance of fate. Whatever happens, will happen.

She stands silent and calm amidst the tall grass. Her wings unfurl slowly, and I realize at this moment that I have never seen them at their full extension. They are broader and wider than she is, twin white feathered canvases that envelop her small frame. Before she had let them out slowly, with a certain hesitation and reluctance that kept them close. But now each wing is filled with purpose and energy. Where there once stood a small dove now a white-winged hawk prepares to take flight. She closes her eyes and clasps her hands as if in prayer and she looks at that moment like a statue I saw in a book long ago.

I let out a breath I hadn't realized I had been holding.

Her wings beat once, twice - then, as they gather power and resolution, they begin to sweep the air with a ferocity that sends a downburst to even where I stand, a few meters away. I have to hold a hand up to my face to protect it from the blasts of winds, and when I look up -

She is aloft.

She is flying higher than I thought possible, almost out of my sight. All I can see is a white shadow spinning and whirling against the starry backdrop of the night sky. I watch in amazement and wonder as she does aerial pirouettes, backflips, dives and swoops...here I was afraid she would not even make it into the air, and here she is almost dancing in the skies. She has gone back to her original form, who she was and was meant to be...an angel.

I run around, screaming like a madman with joy and exultation. The orbital space station is the furthest thing from my mind. She has done it. We have done it. Flight is once again within her reach, and who knows what might come after.

She spirals down, laughing in delight, and this time I am able to catch her as she makes her descent. We spin and whirl together, no less exuberant on the ground than up above.

Finally we come to a stop, both of us exhausted from our motions. I collapse into the ground and she does as well, sending a small storm of feathers up into the air. Her small hand finds mine again as they fall like snow around us, a benediction in white. I give her a reassuring squeeze as I gaze at the heavens above.

Space awaits us - not just me, but humanity as well. And it is all thanks to her. What we have accomplished together is nothing short of a miracle. I turn over and meet her eager and excited gaze.

There is so much more that we will have to do in the future. But for now I am lost in her eyes, and all I want to do is bask in their light for a time...and think of nothing but angels.

A Thousand Miles

★★★★★★

I WAKE UP.

It's another sunny day on the tracks - actually, every day around here is sunny. That's part of the reason I moved here. Don't like clouds, don't like rain, don't like anything besides sun and skies.

I stretch and yawn and roll down and I think of going back to sleep, but I don't. There's too much to do. And if I really feel tired later in the day I can just take a nap.

I bounce out of bed and pull on some coveralls. Going to get dirty later on, so it makes sense to suit up. Breakfast is just whatever I happened to heat up last night. I'm not picky about food - to me it's just an inconvenience that takes time away from more important things.

Like what I'm about to do. I run over to my workstation and I flick on all the buttons at once. The manuals always say to not do that. They want you to do the boring thing and switch them all on one by one, conserve energy, don't strain the system, yadda yadda yadda, but I never do that. I like listening to the thrum of the computers and hearing them all hum to life at once.

The familiar lines of text start scrolling onscreen and I sit back and relax, finishing the last remains of my breakfast. They're just diagnostics - what's booting up where, how, and why, but I love watching them anyway. Calms me down. I finish the remains of my breakfast and lean forwards in anticipation.

There's the flash and blink and pop of the startup and then - there they are. I give them all a wink and wave, even though I know they can't see me. I mean, I know they can pick up my motion on the sensors and cameras, but they can't really SEE me. I mean, they're there and I am here. I won't ever be anything but on the other side of the screen, which makes me kind of sad, but that's the way things are.

I spin my chair around and point to them one by one. Emerson, Cyna, Red, and Rolf. All different colors, all with different words. Out there I sometimes feel alone but I'm never really alone - not with them around me.

They don't talk but all the text on the screen is music to my ears. Emerson is his usual cheerful self. Cyna asks me how many ways I can mess up whatever I'm going to do today. Red doesn't say anything except a "Good Morning" when everyone else is done. And Rolf...you can never really tell with Rolf. I sit and type and type some more. This is the favorite part of my morning - hanging out with the gang.

We talk about what I'm going to do - which is the same as what I do every day. Go out on the tracks of course.

★★★★★★

I don't think the sky has ever been so beautiful as today. I mean, I know I say that every other day. It helps to be positive, y'know?

Sometimes I get a little sad that I don't have anyone to share it with, but then I remember that they're there watching me all the time. I don't have the uplinks necessary to patch them through to the pods when I'm racing, but then again when I'm racing I want to concentrate on the track and what I'm doing. I'll tell them all about it when I get back home.

Today looks like a good day for burning up the tarmac. I don't think I'll try to break any records, just take myself for a spin to two around the track. Keep the wheels oiled up and all that.

I give all the equipment a quick once-over and plug in everything that needs to be plugged in. Then I start the engines. The hum of ignition begins - different than when I start up my systems at home, but also sort of the same. It just makes me happy in a different way. I wait a while for everything to get warmed up, and then I stomp on the accelerator and go.

You know what I like best about racing? It's everything going by so damn fast. It's the feel of the engine beneath your seat thrumming with power. The wind passing you by outside so fast that it leaves streaks against your windscreen. I basically like everything about it, the speed, the rush, the intensity - everything! It's the best.

It's a fairly routine day for me. I don't try any fancy stuff, just hit the straightaways cool and relaxed and take a few turns as fast as I think I can. It's smooth sailing all the time, but then again I'm not pushing any envelopes. Just want to get a feel for all the new additions I installed yesterday...and they're working well, really well in fact. I finish off with a double spin around the last turn just for the hell of it and then it's back home to the gang.

They're all waiting for me to tell them the good news when I get back. Emerson is excited at usual. Cyna doesn't think I handled the second curve around the third right well, but she never thinks I did anything well - that's part of her charm. Red doesn't say anything, but I know that they just means she's happy for me. Rolf points out that I had better adjust my left fender if I want to get more acceleration on the straightaways, and he's right. (as usual)

We're getting there. We're getting there! Everyday there is progress, and that's fantastic. I find myself whistling as I power down the systems, unplug the wires and put everything away. There's data to be analyzed, and adjustments to be made, but today has been a good day - a really good day.

I go to bed dreaming of what I can do tomorrow. If everything works so well today then tomorrow...well, tomorrow is going to be something else.

★★★★★★

Can I break a thousand miles per hour today? I don't know, but I'm going to try. That's half the fun, isn't it?

If we're going to do this, we're going to have to do this properly. I putter around the pod, tweaking settings and adjusting valves. I have to make sure everything is ship-shape and ready to go before I take off the training gloves. Safety first. Doesn't matter what kind of records I break if I end up becoming a red stain somewhere.

They've divided about this course of action, as usual. Emerson is all for it, but then again, he's all for whatever I do. I kind of like having my one-man cheerleading squad, but I also like having Red to bring me back down to Earth, and Cyna for her wit (so, you're gonna make a fool of yourself and bail at 500 miles an hour again today?) and Rolf for his advice - he says to not bother with extra acceleration but go for more control instead...I'll need it on the tougher turns. Everything they say makes sense, even the stuff that doesn't. God I love them all.

Rocket boosters, check. Windscreen layers, check. I think I am getting a little nervous here. I've put every protective measure I know of into place, but you can't be sure about everything, you know? I make a final review, take a deep breath, heave a sigh, and strap myself in. Nothing ventured, nothing gained. The dashboard lights up in front of me and I'm ready to go.

I turn the ignition key and the engine roars to life. I slam on the accelerators and I'm off.

★★★★★★

It didn't really turn out how I wanted it to. I didn't bail at 500 miles per hour (eat that Cyna!) but I didn't crack 900 either. The undercarriage couldn't take the increased strain and so I decided to just abandon the whole idea after the third turning. Safety first.

I was kind of down about it for a while but they all did their best to cheer me up. Even Cyna. Well, what she said was that "you didn't die like I thought you would." Thanks. But I know that's just how she shows that she cares. Red actually said more than a few sentences, and that probably made me feel better that I've been in a long time.

I powered down the pod, collated the data and all that but I didn't really feel like looking at it anymore for a while. I kept on thinking of the thousand miles and how I didn't reach it today. Would I ever reach it? Of course I would. It was just a matter of time. But today wasn't it.

I spent the whole day staring at the clouds instead. I get my best ideas that way. The folk back where I used to live always told me that they looked like animals, or trees, or all that boring stuff, but to me, they always look like more racer pods. I see flanges and boosters and spinning wheels, trails of smoke and engine exhaust, and it just lights me up inside. Usually after about an hour outside I can't wait to get back in and start tinkering with the pod again.

But today they look different. They look a little like birds. Not that I've seen one, of course...this area is about as deserted as they come. But Rolf tells me about them all the time, and I looked them up in his databanks and yeah, I think the clouds today do look those little critters. They have... feathers, that's what they call'em, right? And wings. They use them for flying.

Interesting creatures. They don't even get past like, 50 mph or so? but what they lack of horizontal movement they make up for vertically. I mean, they can fly? That's pretty cool, I must say. I can't fly. Even my pod can't.

I don't think I'm that interested in that though. I mean, I want to go fast, not up. I could probably manage up if I wanted to. I'd have to sacrifice a little thrust for a little lift, and if I deployed the ailerons at an angle I'm sure that my boosters would be able to get me the angle that I needed. But that's not what I want to do, and so I won't.

So many clouds. It's another beautiful day at the tracks.

★★★★★★

Another day, another retrofitting. This time I know what was the problem. I'm certain of it, in fact. It's the wheel casing. It's just not strong enough to handle the extra power I'm pumping out, which is why it started shaking, and that was why the phase connectors couldn't handle the pressure, and why the undercarriage couldn't take the strain and that led to...well, basically I have to fix the wheel casing.

With what, though? I need something strong, but flexible enough to bend and not break when I really put the pedal to the metal. I think about various ways around it...I could temper the whole chassis with a phase distortion. That would get it to where I wanted but then it wouldn't interface well with the rest of the machinery. I could maybe just reroute the central power circuit back onto itself while bypassing the reflex valve, which... would probably be too dangerous. Even for me.

Wait, wait...wait. I have it. I think I actually have it! It's not the wheel casing at all. It's the regulator! I just need to release the limit on the regulator for a few seconds - just a few, while I'm hitting the straightaway after the third turn and before the fourth. That's when I get the maximum thrust and if I time it juuuuuuuuust right I think I'll be able to get the last few ounces of power I need. In fact I'm sure of it! Why didn't I think of this before? I guess you can't rush genius.

Red tells me that I'm going overboard with this idea, which is strange for her. Rolf actually agrees with her once. Emerson thinks whatever I'm doing is right (as usual) and Cyna...Cyna is silent for once. I keep on thinking she's swapped places with Red but no, Cyna's not saying anything and Red is. I smile but I go right back to what I'm doing. I have this one in the bag and I know it.

They chatter on as I yank out cable after cable and plug them back in. God I love my family. I have no idea what I'd do without them. Go insane and smash the pod and myself into something most probably. I work through the night, cutting sheet metal into the shapes I need, debugging the databanks, and tweaking the transistor arrays. Tomorrow is the day, but we won't get there without a LOT more preparation.

I go to sleep happy and satisfied. We're almost there, no matter what they say. Almost there.

★★★★★★

Alright, time to have another go at that thousand mile mark! I bounce out of bed and almost forget to eat breakfast, but Rolf reminds me that I can't race on an empty stomach. Good old Rolf. I can always rely on him to take care of me. The rest chime in with their remarks soon after...Emerson is all gogogo! Cyna is cautiously optimistic (a new mode for her!) and Red doesn't say anything, which is normal for her again. I'm kind of relieved at her silence actually.

I'm so excited I can't even sit still. Or assemble anything properly. But I somehow manage to calm myself enough to go over the systems slowly and methodically, testing each one by one.

But it doesn't work. I don't even get to 750 this time. The wheel casings are doing just fine and I'm sure I have enough thrust to the accelerator but I don't even get to the point where I need to disengage the limiters. I did everything the same as yesterday...but I'm at least a hundred miles slower. Why? I don't understand.

I'm not even down this time, just curious. What isn't working? What CAN'T be working? I've checked the figures with all of them and input them into multiple simulations. They all agree I'm on the right track with this one (no pun intended) but it doesn't seem to be panning out like it should.

I take the pod on two more rounds around the track just for the heck of it. Nope, still too slow. Far, FAR too slow.

You know what? I think it's me. I maybe it's my fragile human self that is just too chicken. I don't dare to go as fast as I need to. The plan is to get to 900 and then let loose, really let her rip...but I can't even do that. I need to be wilder. More reckless. Throw caution to the wind and just GO.

I've wished more than once that I could be like them. Sitting there, connected to everything, with all that knowledge and processing power at your disposal. No need to get up, to sleep, to eat, to do all those messy things biological organisms have to do. Just compute faster that I ever could.

But then if I was like them I couldn't race. And I couldn't go out and see the clouds and get ideas about how to race better. I don't know which would hurt more. I guess I'm happy being where I am, even if I don't crack a thousand miles.

★★★★★★

It's another bright and sunny today, but somehow I don't feel like racing. Or tinkering with the pod. Or doing much of anything. But I never don't feel like racing. What's wrong with me?

I do what I do when I'm confused about anything - I go ask them. Emerson tells me it's just a funk and it will pass. I sure hope so. Cyna says not to think too much or I'll hurt my head. Thanks. Red is silent as usual and Rolf doesn't say anything either.

Nothing's helping. I just feel so...so...depressed. And I never feel depressed, at least not since I moved out here.

I'm going to go look at the clouds.

★★★★★★

It's another sunny day, good for cloud watching. Like I said, every day is sunny out here.

I'm waiting for inspiration to come but nothing turns up. Just birds as usual. More birds - big ones, small ones, thin ones, fat ones. All kinds.

I sigh and I feel more than a little frustrated. Birds are ok. Birds are fine. But what I need is more power, more speed, more intensity, not these feathery critters. Like I said before, I want to go fast, not up.

I rub my eyes and roll around on the sand, then roll around some more and rub my eyes again. Nope, not working. Still clouds that look like birds. Not a racer pod or thruster in sight.

I spend an hour or so more outside and then I decide to call it a day and go back.

★★★★★★

It's raining. No racing for me today. I guess I could go and check on everything but then, I've already checked everything a thousand times (ha, ha) already. There's nothing left to adjust or tweak that I haven't already adjusted or tweaked enough.

They're worried about me, I can tell. Rolf is silent (now HE'S giving me the silent treatment? it'll be Emerson next...) Red only says something once every hour or so. Cyna berates me as usual but her voice has lost some of its sting. Emerson tells me that I'm doing good, I'm doing great - I'll hit a thousand miles tomorrow! - but I think both of us know that that's just empty talk.

The rain matches my mood. It pours down in thick sheets of water and I stare at it glumly. I feel like the shelter is a giant racer pod...one that doesn't even do 1 mph, let alone a thousand.

What am I doing wrong? What I do need to change? I think and think and think but nothing comes to mind. All that happens is that I feel worse than ever.

I decide to go to sleep. No use sitting here staring at water come down from the skies. It's about as helpful as those damn birds.

★★★★★★

Nothing's working. Nothing's working! I'm never going to get past a thousand, and I'm never going to get out of this bad mood, and I'm never going to...arrgggh, screw it.

I fling my spanner down in frustration. They all don't say a word. They're probably as upset and confused as I am. I've never been like this. Never.

I mean, I've had setbacks before. There was the time the carburetor went kaput. Boy, that took me more than a week to fix. And the other time when the pulse arrays went crazy...that was nuts. They all had to pitch in and we worked from morning to night to debug all the goddamn things. But when we were done we were back in racing in a jiffy.

So yeah, I'm used to things going wrong. All part of the plan. But it's never been like this before...I mean, it's like I'm stuck and I don't even know why. This is even worse than the depression from before.

I try to sleep - could be just that I'm tired maybe? I toss and I turn for a few hours but sleep isn't happening either. I get up, bleary-eyes and irritable, and stomp outside.

Of all of them Red tries this time. She tells me that I should just take it easy, that things will look better tomorrow. What does she know? She just sits there with the rest all day, she doesn't need to get up or fix things or...now I'm getting angry at them? Ok I know I've really lost it this time.

I shoot them all a pained look but all I get is the glow of the screens in return. No one says anything. I think they don't know what to say either. I don't blame them...I don't know what to DO either.

Maybe I'll go outside.

★★★★★★

No clouds today either. Clear skies - great for racing, but that's out of the question. Sigh. Just my luck, huh?

I sit myself down and look at the sky but I find myself thinking about home. Not that home. I mean, home is here. That's why I picked this spot - far away from anyone and anything, where I could be with them and do whatever I wanted. That's home. But there was another home before this one, not that I call it home anyway, but it USED to be home, and...I'm confused myself.

They wanted me to get married, to settle down. Have kids, I think. I can't quite remember anymore. But I didn't care for any of those things. All I wanted to do was race.

It's not really clear but I think I'm remembering a few other things as well. They wanted me to do something...some things? Fix things, I think. We didn't have enough food, and they wanted me to do something to some machine or another...I can't recall and I don't really care. All I wanted to do was race, and go faster, and then one day when things got bad enough I just ran off and here I am.

I never think about home...I mean, that place I used to come from. I'm usually just too busy to think about anything besides racing. And my family.

It's all so confusing and I don't really like it. All I really want to do is crack that goddamn thousand mile mark.

★★★★★★

Okay, today is the day. I can feel it. It's going to happen. I'm going to get to a thousand and it's going to be great. I feel strangely exhilarated and I think that's good...it's like nothing I've ever felt before. Which is good, I think.

I make sure I do everything properly. Safety first. I check the wheel casings and the regulator and the pulse array and well, everything. Then I run some simulations and I psyche myself up and I check everything a second time again. It all looks good. This is it. This is it.

They don't seem as excited as I am, which is strange. Then again they've been behaving strangely lately. Just two nights ago I could have sworn that I heard them talking to each other while I was asleep. Cyna isn't as sarcastic as usual, and even Emerson doesn't talk, and Red...what's wrong with everyone? I have no idea.

But when I look at the pod all of that vanishes. I'm gonna break that thousand miles today, I just know it.

I strap myself in and I am so excited that I almost don't remember to give everything a final once-over. Or adjust the limiters on the regulator. Or make sure the windshield layer is intact. I don't know why I'm so sure that I am going to make it today, but I am.

The first few rounds go smoothly enough. I start at around 500 no problem, and with each round it just keeps getting better. 600, then 700, then 750...the casings are holding, the undercarriage is fine and the engine is working on all cylinders. I'm happy. I'm excited...ecstatic even. If this keeps up I'll get to 1000 with no problems at all.

A few more rounds and we get to the redzone...900 and climbing. I stall out at around 950 but that's what I've been waiting for. I punch the button and the limiters come off and I hit a curve and then I turn and I come out onto a straightaway. 920, 921, 943, 955...it's all coming together and I can't wait to tell them the news back home and -

- then all hell breaks loose. I knew the wheel casings couldn't take the strain. The limiters come off alright, but back blast from the exhaust is just too strong and it breaks the connection to the central pulse array. The feedback fries almost everything that's in the area - which is basically the entire onboard system. Of course I don't know any of this at the time. All I know is that one moment everything is going fine and the next I go spinning out of control and I'm hanging onto the wheel for dear life as sparks fly everywhere. The engine goes haywire and the internal stresses start to tear apart the entire pod and I can't do anything because I'm too busy trying to stay alive. I careen helplessly into a nearby tree with a huge bang and before I know it flame starts licking at the edge of the windscreens. I struggle to get out but I'm afraid it's going to be too late -

- and at the last moment the safety systems kick in. Flame retardant spews for a nozzle I didn't even know I installed and the fire's gone. But the pod is a wreck. T struggle to get myself out of it and I finally manage to extricate myself from the mass of twisted metal it has become.

I almost can't bear to look at it again but I force myself to and...yeah. It's worse than I thought. The damage is so severe there is no way to even begin to fix it. I just stand there for a while, looking at it in stunned silence. Then I go back home.

★★★★★★

But I don't want to go back home. I ended up going where I usually go to look at the clouds...except that there are no clouds today. I plonk myself down and feel sorry for myself.

What am I going to do? I mean, the pods ruined. Even Cyna will be sad for me. Probably. If she doesn't chew me out first. I can't even think of what the others will say.

So why don't I want to go home? Either home, I mean. I don't know. All I know is that I feel worse than I've ever felt in my entire life. No pod, no thousand miles, no nothing.

What was I thinking...it was dumb of me. Stupid. I should have found a safer way to go about doing things. Slow and steady...who am I kidding? Slow and steady would have taken forever. I went for it and I crashed and burned. Simple as that.

After a few hours I eventually do make myself go back. If it rains, I'm going to be stuck out here with no shelter and no pod and no nothing. At least back home they're there for me.

★★★★★★

They're all glad to see me. They don't show it - they can't show it, more like - but it's obvious. I'm glad to see them too. No one says anything at first. Which is good...I think if I heard anything from them I'd just burst out crying. They let me get some food and sit down a bit and generally feel normal again.

I sit down and mope and they all do their best to help me get through it. I'm so down that I can't remember exactly what everyone said, but they all did their best, I'm sure of it.

What should I do? I have no idea. I sit around a bit and eventually I go to bed. There's nothing else TO do. Sleep comes a lot faster and more easily than I think it would. It's probably because I'm so tired.

★★★★★★

What's a girl to do when her only hope and reason for existence goes up in flames? Why, build another one, of course.

I surprise myself (and them, of course) by how fast I bounce back. I wake up the next morning with a burning desire to get back on the tracks, and I start work on a new pod minutes after breakfast. I have all the parts, and if I go back to the wreckage of the crash I can find enough materials to make things easier. So that's what I do. I go back and grit my teeth and scrounge up whatever spare parts I can and go to it.

They are all largely silent on the matter. Red does tell me not to work too hard, and Rolf offers a hint here and there, but they all don't say much of anything else. Even Emerson doesn't say anything (he finally got his turn!) I think they want to let me sort through it on my own, and I appreciate it.

I spend the better part of 3 weeks working like a demon. I weld metal and splice arrays with a speed that amazes even me. Slowly a new pod begins to take shape - first the exoskeleton, a thin frame of phase distorted metal. They I slap on some plates, connect the computers, add wheels...it's one thing after another. I know how to do it, I just gotta go it better than I have ever done before. I don't even ask them for any help. it's something I have to do on my own.

I even whistle while I work. It's hard work but it's what I want to do. I want to race - I'm surer of that that anything - and I can't do it without a pod. So I gotta make another. It's that simple. Some part of me is I'm really not sure if I ought be doing this much work when the crash is still so recent in my memory, but I think that if I don't keep myself busy I'll probably fall into another funk again. Working is definitely the lesser of two evils.

★★★★★★

I had a dream today. I never have dreams. Not since moving out here.

I was running to - or was it running from? - somewhere, and I was going faster and faster and it was great. It was like being in the pod, except that I was outside, and Emerson was cheering me on and Cyna was telling me I was doing good and Red was shouting (shouting? Red?) and Rolf was saying something that I couldn't quite hear and I was going faster than I ever had gone before and -

- suddenly I was a bird. But not one of those normal, boring ones. I had wings of steel and plumes of fire and I was going fast, incredibly fast, easily 700, then 800, then 900 and the limiters were off and I was going to -

and then I woke up. I tried to go back to sleep but I couldn't. Still, it was the best dream ever.

Weeks pass faster than I realize. It seems like one day I am still fine-tuning some schematics and attaching the blasted wheel casings (always have to watch out for those!) and the next day I'm done. It's done!

I go over and stare at it. Everything is ready to go. It's as good as I can make it, probably even be better than before. I learned from the crash and I've managed to integrate everything together into a faster (hopefully) and leaner model.

I look at the pod. Then I look outside, past the garage door, into the wide open skies and green fields outside. Then I look at the pod again.

Maybe...maybe it's just not worth it. I can't believe I'm thinking this but I am. Maybe I should just call it quits. Hang in the towel and never get into a pod again. I mean, it's a miracle that I haven't even crashed before that time. That I'm still alive. And I have to think about all of them too. If I die...then all of them will be sad, real sad.

I feel something that I've never felt before. What is it... fear? No. I never feel afraid, not even when I ran, not even when I crashed. Well, maybe then, but that was more fear that I wouldn't get to a thousand. It's different. I don't know what it is but for some reason it doesn't bug me. I still don't know what I'm feeling though.

I go outside.

★★★★★★

The clouds are...the clouds look weird today. They don't look like anything. Just clouds. No birds or pods or thrusters or wings. Just clouds.

I'm not sure what to do or think or feel, so I just continue looking up at the sky. The wind picks up and sighs against my face and I wonder why I've never felt it before. I guess I was going too fast? And when the windshields are up you can't actually feel the wind, you can only see it going by. Who knew that it would feel like this? Like someone touching you so quickly that it was gone before it began. A gentle ripple against your skin that's so fast you can't see it before you blink.

I suddenly wonder what they would all say if they saw the sky. Or the clouds. Would they see birds or racer pods? What would they say? Emerson would be all for it, he would say... I have no idea what he would say. Or any of them.

I could never manage to drag them all out here anyway. Too many wires. And I could never bring the outdoors back inside.

I just sit back and relax and daydream...yeah, I guess that's what I'm doing. I'm daydreaming, just without getting any ideas this time. I reach out a lazy hand and I see the sunlight come in through my splayed fingers.

How long from here to the sun? To the clouds? I'm not sure...I guess I could run some simulations but I don't have the data to do that. So I'll just guess. A few hundred...no, too small. A thousand miles? Maybe more. A thousand thousand miles.

And long would it take? A thousand thousand miles at a thousand miles an hour...so a thousand hours. That's a long time. I'd run out of food by then, and water. And I'd have to leave them all behind too. Not to mention I'd need a lot of lift to even get off the ground and go that far.

What am I thinking? I'm never going to be able to do that. I've thought about this before, haven't I? Adjust the ailerons and the boosters to point upwards, but then I won't have enough thrust to get off the ground. Maybe if I turn it sideways? Naah, that's a dumb idea. How about if I feed the flow into the regulator instead, and then from there I remove the limiters, and then the pulse array should...wait.

That's it...that's it! Ideas start flowing into my head all of a sudden. Repurpose the boosters. Strip away the wheel casings for less weight. I never needed the damn things anyway.

Increase the boost factor of the exhaust. It might work. It just might work.

Why not both? Why not go fast AND go up? Why stay on the ground when I can fly? I can barely restrain myself. I bound off the hill and head for home.

I can hardly wait to get back and tell them the good news. Emerson will be so happy for me. I know Cyna will have a snarky comment to make but I'm sure even she can see the potential in what I'm suggesting...Red may say something, or she may not. And I can never tell with Rolf.

I wonder whether I'll see any birds up there.

★★★★★★

Rusty Rose

RUSTY ROSE

The sky spread slate-grey above the city, and a seamless mass of traffic wound its way like a river through the roads.

Richard Grant slumped back in his chair after a hard day of work. Sighing, he reached up to loosen his tie, at the same time tapping the console at his side to order a drink. He could afford to relax. He'd just finished a entire week of signing, wining and dining the hardest-nosed businessmen the city had to offer, including hammering out a contract with Harrelson and Co - who seemed determined not to let him get what he considered his fair share of the proceedings. You would think he was trying to pull a fast one over them, the way they carried on.

But that wasn't how Endrane Corporation did things. It had been a fair deal - the only kind he ever inked. He had even written in a clause indemnifying them against any kind of suit from him. If that wasn't fair he didn't know. What did they want, full corporate immunity? He could just seem them sitting there smiling at him, the fat cats in their suits

Mentally scowling at himself - he hated thinking about work - he wound down the protective shield on the windows. He'd been told by his bodyguard not to do that many times, but sometimes he got bored of staring at the black screens instead of glass. Besides, he told himself, he just wanted to look out for a while, take his mind off things.

Outside were rows upon rows of, a vista of unbroken concrete. All his. All factories in his name. He hadn't gotten out of the industrial area of the city yet - it would be a good twenty miles or so before the scenery would consist of other things besides an endless procession of smokestacks and industrial buildings.

He wound the screen down again.

The next five minutes were spent in silence. He sipped his drink carelessly, letting his thoughts wander. It was a good thing he had gotten the Bioflux installed in the car - he generally wanted one the moment he stepped in, and having one made beforehand would just spoil the taste. He dialed another one up on the console and finished the first. The journey back from his office always made him thirsty.

It would be a while more before he reached home. As the minutes dragged on he realized, not without some surprise, that he was slowly but surely growing bored. Usually it was just one thing after another - meetings, lunches, company obligations. But today it seemed that he was presented with that rarity of rarieties - free time.

To verify it for himself beyond all doubt, he mentally ticked off the things in his mind. No more meetings tomorrow. No lunches either. There was something to be cleared up about the leases in Seramel contract, but he would get his secretary and staff to handle that - he paid them more than enough, anyway. Yes, that was all there was to do.

Amazing. He relaxed back into the plush synthetic leather of his seat. Nothing else to do, not for the moment, and not for the immediate future either. He finished his second drink and laid back again, letting himself mull on the prospect of his newfound free time for a while.

Now...now was the time to relax for a while. He certainly deserved it. The time for relaxation...and the time for pleasure.

Before he knew it, his fingers were dancing over the touchpad for the phone, and soon enough, the cool chime from the receptionist droid was telling him that yes, his request had been processed, and that yes, they would have someone waiting for him at his residence in the evening, thank you very much for your patronage.

He settled down to wait, and the rest of the ride passed quickly.

★★★★★★

The limousine turned and wound its way through the streets, down past the liner trains and the transrails. He saw the new ones being installed - they would reportedly reduce travel time down this at this area by at least half. Not that he cared. Those were for the commoners, though who could not afford their own private vehicles and had to use what meagre offerings the city could dole out to its less fortunate inhabitants. And out beyond that would be the spaceport, with its gleaming arches and tall spires.

It all passed him by so quickly he didn't register it. He saw the same scenery every day, and even if his mind hadn't been preoccupied with other, more pleasant things, he wouldn't have paid it any heed. Lost in thought, he was still musing while the car slowed and headed down the lanes leading to where he lived. When was the last time he had some time to himself? Too long.

Soon enough, the mansion came into view. He scowled as he passed the entrance. The gardens were in a terrible state. He saw two rosebushes out of place, and at least half of them were the blue of the last season, instead of the red that he had expressedly specified that he wanted. His trained eye scanned the flowers and his frown grew even more pronounced.

He would have to speak to Mrs Harrison about it, get it fixed. It wouldn't do to have people - clients, especially - come in commenting on the state of his gardens. He ran a tight ship here at Endrane, and he expected each and every aspect of that to be perfect – or at least come close – from his suit to the taste of the filtered waters and the gardens. Especially the gardens. Real roses were hard to come by, and he wanted each and every visitor to his estate to know that he had the finest collection of them on the planet.

But that was another concern for another time. Today... today was for pleasure. The car swung into the empty alcove near his chambers and he got out, loosening his tie as he did so. Time to meet his guest.

★★★★★★

He was early. But then again, he was always early. A working habit not easily broken...in his business it always paid to be early, never late. You never knew what would happen, and it was always good to take the extra time to be prepared. So even when he wasn't working he was always made sure to be more than on time. It didn't make sense to leave anything to chance.

He poured himself a stiff drink from the dispenser in his room and settled in to wait. After a while, she arrived.

She wasn't quite what he had expected. He paid the company to provide variety, but she was different than all the other girls that he had ordered before. It wasn't the pale red hair and the flat eyes that seemed to stare through him. It was something else...something that he couldn't quite pinpoint.

"You're new." It was a lame, obvious statement, and he knew it. But that was one thing about talking to an android, especially one paid for a service – you didn't need to be polite, didn't need to indulge in meaningless societal niceties; not if you didn't want to. It was almost always "just business". Oh, certainly there were higher-class models, and personal servants owned by the rich which you always had to accord at least a modicum of respect to, but, for the most part, you could dispense with the formalities.

That was one of the things he liked. The other - he didn't even know what it might be himself. But with them - normally, even in the most mundane of corporate settings, he would inadvertently say something that would cause even the most bored and jaded socialite to roll her eyes and seek more pleasant (or at least eloquent) company. But these girls? They wouldn't mind in the least. After all, they weren't human.

What was it about them? Their eyes? Their face? Even their manner of speech and movement - there was always something, something that nagged at the edges of his consciousness but that he could never quite put his finger on.

It wasn't that they weren't real. "Real" as in alive...it wasn't something so obvious. So crass. Nothing to do with the texture of their skin, the color of their eyes. The way the moved? The too-quick blinking of their eyes that even the best scientists could never remove? It had to be something else, but he could never quite figure out what.

It didn't matter, though. Right now she was standing in front of him, waiting, her handbag carried discreetly close to her, veil shading her eyes. She was dressed simply – a red dress that set off her eyes, and a cobalt blue sash over that. He thought the rose in her hair was a nice touch.

"What's your name?" he asked.

"Rachel." the girl replied. A simple name. He held out his hand, and she followed him.

Along the way to his rooms, they made small talk - inconsequential, completely unnecessary dialogue. To his amazement he found himself stammering at one point, but she just smiled and blinked once, twice - and his embarrassment vanished. As they neared his elevator he was filled with sudden vain bravery and opened the door for her as they stepped into it, the ruthless businessman turned charming, even gallant.

He remembered that once he even caught himself offering one of them a drink - it had seemed like the proper thing to do - and then had ridiculed himself for his foolishness. They were paid to come here...he didn't need to treat them THAT well. And more to the point, they couldn't drink. It would just stain their systems and then he would have to pay a hefty cleaning fee.

Yes, he didn't need to do that. He could he wanted to, though. He could be anything - even cruel, even sadistic. He had heard that outright brutality was quite popular these days, among the rich. Apparently it was in vogue in some circles to damage them so much that they had to be taken back to the repair shop - only to be put back the next day without a scratch. The benefits of taking your wanton excesses out on a machine.

He mulled on it a bit longer as the walk to his rooms - always long, he preferred to live as far away from the main estate as possible - continued. He surprised himself by having more placid tastes. In his office he would insist that his water be served just so, his meals exactly on time. He had fired servants for less, screamed at them for failing to inform him of anything. It didn't matter - the staff could take it. It was even expected, for someone of his position.

With the girls, though, there was no violence, no demands or perverse whims to be catered to. With them he was content to simply flip through the catalogs carelessly, selecting this one or that one, even asking for advice or suggestions from the staff once in a while. The company did its job well - there was always something to appeal to him, something fresh and new, interesting enough to intrigue but not tawdry or overly-familiar. He supposed that somewhere there was a psych profile of him, somewhere in a room full of computers where they had matched his tastes and personality to exactly what they thought would please him. It didn't bother him as much as he thought it would. As long as he was happy, he would pay them their fee.

They had walked far from the gardens by then. It would just be a short way past the offices, and then they would be at

44

their destination. He never took the shuttle with the girls – he always preferred to walk. It lengthened the pleasant time he would spend with them.

He turned to address her. "I'm sorry my rooms are so far, Rachel."

"It's fine, Mr Grant." He noticed that this one had just the hint of on accent – from where and of what, he couldn't quite place – and it delighted him strangely. He hadn't known he liked accents before.

Ten more minutes or so of walking and then they were there. He got the passcard out, and with a silent hiss, the door slid open. He gestured to the bedroom, and she followed.

★★★★★★

Once again there was no fumbling, no awkwardness. He was only aware of undressing hastily and glimpsing her fair, white body before she beckoned to him and they both moved onto the bed.

He had done this many times before, with many different girls, but with her it was all a confused jumble of images and sensations. At times he didn't know exactly what he was doing – putting it in or taking it out, thrusting or grinding or turning this way and that. She was on top, and then the next minute he was, and through the haze of pleasure that assaulted him he could hear her faint moans and his own low grunts.

At some points he was tensing under her expert ministrations, and at others he was guiding her as if suddenly she was as innocent as a virgin maid. So many sensations – hard, soft, and everything in between – but all thoroughly pleasurable.

Then it was over – he didn't know quite when – and he relaxed, spent, on the bed. He felt her leave her side of the mattress but continued to drift in and out of consciousness in a light, heady daze.

It was only when he heard the music that he sat up.

45

"What are you doing?" Another stupid question - it was obvious just from looking that she had started to play the piano. From the glance she gave him - a quick flick of the eyes - it seemed that she knew the question was rhetorical, and that it didn't matter to her playing. Her fingers and hands danced over the keys, faster than any human hands could ever be, drawing from them a beautiful, haunting melody.

He hated it. Hated it with such violent intensity that suddenly he found himself wishing for something to throw at her - anything - at her, at the blasted piano and the damned music. He cast around for a clock or nearby lamp to hurl at the blithely playing android but turned up with nothing. Of course, the room had been swept clean before they even entered it. But the music...he hated it and it had to stop, immediately.

He strode to her, ready to wrench her hands away from the keys if need be, but just as he was about to raise his hands, he stopped. He stood over her, his face a mask of control. "Stop playing." His voice had sunk to a low undertone.

She stopped. Her eyes met his for a moment and then dropped back to the keys.

"This is a nice piano." she said, letting her fingers skate over the keys, almost but not quite touching them, skipping from one to another - black-white-white-black-black - with something approaching tenderness. "But it's not quite in tune yet."

"I don't care." He was still barely restraining his anger. He wanted to reach out, to snap that perfect neck, to slam his fist into the graceful, petite frame, but somehow he kept a hold on himself. "Don't you dare play it again."

"Why?" She looked up again, and her eyes were simple, guileless. "Don't you like music?"

"No." It wasn't quite the truth. He didn't dislike music - but then again he didn't much like it either. He had attended some concerts as part of charity events, and he found them pleasant in a vague, distant kind of way - bright lights in the background, pretty girls on stage. But he hadn't really paid attention then.

But her playing was different. The music and that damn piano. It had roused something in him - a cold, dark anger that later he would find himself almost frightened and chastised by. Now...now he only wanted to get her out of the house before he did something he would later regret.

"Leave. Now." He watched as she gathered her things - silently, gracefully - and left, closing the door without a sound.

Then he slumped down on the bed, alone. He would need a drink.

★★★★★★

He tried not to think of the incident after that. Of course, it had put him into an especially foul mood the next day, and his frustration and anger continued to dog him all into the next week. Work, usually simply just routine at best and tiresome at worst, became a dreary chore, and he delegated what he could to his subordinates, leaving the rest for his staff to clear up.

The next week he called the agency up again. Send someone up, he said. No, he had no preferences. Yes, he was sure. Yes, he trusted their expertise implicitly. Thank you very much.

The next day another girl arrived, just at the time he had specified. She was blue-haired and short, with pale lips and pierced ears − quite, quite different from Rachel. He went through the motions - the stammering, the initial nervousness, the act itself and the sweet, cool, aftermath.

But somehow it wasn't the same. Two days after he could barely remember the girl - the color of her hair, her name, her dress. He supposed that he had enjoyed himself - the agency always did a good job, but the pleasure seemed distant, faraway. Different.

The next week he called back again, and they sent someone else. But this time he enjoyed himself even less, if that was possible.

His foul mood persisted at work, and after 2 months had passed he began to contemplate other vices. His was considered a quiet, unobtrusive one by his peers. It didn't involve killing, or maiming. No ruined lives, no bloodsport or addiction. It was simple, discreet - thought of by some almost quaint.

He tried. From a chance conversation at a ball somewhere, he was told that carrying on with drugged human females was quite in vogue nowadays. There was a muscle stimulant so powerful that it made the sensations of climax So he dutifully, almost by rote, went to purchase one, and asked his staff to acquire. But when it came to the actual act itself he found it pathetic, almost disgusting. He had surprised himself again.

In the end he was back to where he was. For some reason that he himself couldn't quite fathom...he wanted her. Not anything else - not anyone else. Only her.

★★★★★★

It grew to be almost an obsession. He found himself thinking of her at the most inappropriate times – in meetings, during worker inspections, while he was discussing the latest figures with his financiers. They would rise to mind unbidden - the memory of her red eyes and dress, the rose she wore in her hair, the sensation of her cool white fingers running down the length of his leg. He wished to be rid of the images almost as much as he reveled in them.

Until one day he came back from a particularly long and vicious meeting to find a message waiting for him. His secretary informed him that it hadn't come from the usual channels, but that it didn't seem to be bugged in any way. He nodded curtly and said that he would read it in his office.

It was from her. How she'd managed to find his private number, or been able to make a direct call, he didn't know - but it also didn't matter. He just wanted to read the message.

It was simple enough. It stated how she had enjoyed his company, and how she would like to see him again. She wasn't working for the agency that he had contacted her through anymore, but if he wanted, he could get in touch with her new employers and they would see about contacting her. She would be delighted to come back to visit, but only if she could play the piano.

He spent some time in silence, reading it once, twice, three times. He had told his secretary to hold all calls, even urgent ones. "Mr Grant is indisposed right now." - that was what she should tell anyone who asked.

"Wasn't working for them anymore..." he didn't know quite what to make of that. How could androids "not work"? As far as he knew, it wasn't a choice for them. Maybe there was something he didn't understand about her, or about the agency. He had heard of black market chips that could override the control circuits of any android...it smelled fishy, and completely not the kind of thing that the head of a multi-billion corporation should get himself involved in.

He could get to the bottom of this matter. He could call up experts, specialists, even detectives. With the amount of money at his disposal, he could get in touch with a top-notch roboticist, ask him questions. He would be able to explain what the message meant, and what Rachel was really asking of him.

But he didn't. He felt suddenly tired, conscious of a great weariness bearing down on him. He had had enough of calling this or that person up, of asking questions and getting few answers. He had enough of that at work. And then, when the fatigue was too great to bear, diverting himself with this or that idle pursuit, only to be left alone and spiritless at the end of the day.

So he found himself writing a short and simple reply. Yes, he would like to see her again. She was welcome to come back at any time if only she called in advance. The piano would be made available, but she should not expect it to be tuned.

He debated with himself on how to end it. "Thank you" seemed too prosaic. "Sincerely" would be false. In the end, he simply signed his name and sent it off.

★★★★★★

The wait was longer than he had expected. It was three weeks before he received a reply, three weeks of interminable waiting and exhausted anticipation. This time, though, there was no pleasant expectation, no thoughts of an evening that would be spent lost in her pale white body.

He spent the time in work and what seemed like endless trips to and from the office. He answered call after call and went to meeting after meeting, trying to put all thoughts of the android girl out of his mind.

But finally the reply came. If it was alright with him, she would visit next week, and come around in the evening. She looked forwards to seeing him again. She would be wearing a white dress this time, with a lily in her hair. No mention was made of the piano.

Next week came, and after a restless day at work, he arrived home to find her waiting for him in the gardens. They said nothing to each other and simply walked in silence to his rooms.

★★★★★★

It was different this time. Half-remembered images of their previous interaction mixed with sharp sensations of the present, and he relaxed into her even as he tensed against her cool body. He was faintly aware of her voice in his ear coaxing him on to greater heights, and he tried to respond as best as he was able until finally they both reached their peaks and he fell into a deep, exhausted sleep.

He awoke to find her sitting at the piano in the state of half-undress, a silken ribbon draped carelessly over a bared thigh. She smiled at him and began to play.

He bore it the best he could. Grimacing, he turned away and stared out the window. The melody leapt and danced with frivolous glee, and it was obvious to any listener that she was more than expert at the instrument, her hands coaxing lilting notes from the keys deftly. But all that beauty and grace was lost on him. All he wanted was for the music to stop.

In an effort to take his mind off her infernal playing he continued to stare out the window. He saw the rows and rows of corporate housing and he wondered, not for the first time, how the other people in the city lived. The ones who had not the resources to afford mansions and roses and android playthings. What did they do for work? For leisure? Some of them undoubtedly worked at Endrane, and others made the car that he took to work and back every morning - or did robots do that? In that case, someone had to make those same robots. Where did the flow of industry stop and begin?

The thoughts managed to stop the flow of notes to his ears and he was perversely grateful for that. He continued to think in the same vein for a while. If people made the robots that maintained the city, then some must also have had a hand in the creation of androids...unless those didn't live in corporate housing. If they were skilled enough to create girls like Rachel, they most probably lived in mansions like his own, which meant that...he suddenly realized that there was no more music.

When he turned around to look, she had left.

★★★★★★

But she came back the next week, and the week after that. Without any letters or words being exchanged, they had fallen into an unspoken agreement of sorts. She would come in the evening, and they would make love, and afterwards she would play the piano while he looked out through the window.

It became a routine. What had stared with stammers and unknowns had become a sense of open familiarity. The second month he even struck up a conversation with her - about what, he couldn't quite recall. Something mundane and completely uninteresting.

She had replied politely and noncommittally, and he didn't remember what she said either, but crinkling of her cheeks in laughter and the too-red of her lips as she raised a hand to them - those he did remember, and for a long time.

Weeks came and passed, and one day he even had the piano tuned. She hadn't seemed to notice, but then again, maybe she couldn't even tell. He had no idea how androids heard music, and somehow she had been able to play it perfectly many times despite

He lost track of time. How long had she been coming here? It could have been months, or even a year. He didn't know anymore. Everything was on his company records, of course, but as usual as it was with her he felt disinclined to check…to do nothing expect spend time with this strange android girl who had so captured his attention. If it wasn't for her penchant for piano playing, he would have bought the rights to her from her employer (whoever it was) a long time ago. As it was, he was content to have her come over each week where they would make their exchange and part till the next week. And the next.

★★★★★★

On evening on a whim, he has asked her to join him outside his window on the balcony for a drink, and he had been surprised as her ready acquiescence.

They looked out over the city, and he allowed himself to imagine what she might be thinking. Did androids dream? Or wonder? Her face was the same expressionless mask as always - pretty, but bereft of any feeling or emotion. How she could look so, and be so passionate in bed, was truly a wonder of science and engineering.

He wasn't sure if that was what so entranced him. Maybe it was. Before he could pursue that thought further, she surprised him with a sudden question.

"Your drinks...?"

"They're non-alcoholic." In response to her raised eyebrow he let out a short bark of laughter. "Yeah, it's a joke alright. Near impossible to find genuine alcohol nowadays. The most they have is some artificial or chemical stimulant. Works well, apparently gives the same buzz, but without the side effects. I can't do without it." The last was true. He couldn't remember the last day he had gone through without a drink or two. He supposed that he could do without them for a day - or even a week - if he tried (they were supposed to be non-addictive after all) but he had never dared to try.

And why should he? A man of his wealth could drink them all day and afford the regenerative treatment if any of his organs should fail from overimbibing.

She smiled, and went back to playing the piano, and he went back to staring out of the window, thinking.

★★★★★★

Another visit came soon on the heels of the last. He had grown inured to the piano playing, or at least he thought he had. He simply drank, or stared out the window, and somehow he was able to tune it out at least partially.

It was amazing how...familiar they had become over the last few months. She knew his schedule like clockwork now, and she came in

Slowly it began to grate on him. Not her company – that was as delightful as always. They had dinners together occasionally, and when he could spare the time, even lunches.

It was the damned piano playing. He knew the terms of their agreement quite well - sex in exchange for playing the piano. He had inked enough contracts to know that if he broke the agreement he would get none of what he wanted. But there were some things he just could not stand, and the piano was one of them.

One evening the strange, sudden anger seized him again and he spat out the words harshly.

"Could you stop playing?"

She paused, fingers frozen in mid-stroke. "Excuse me, Mr Grant?" He had never been able to get him to call him Richard, even though he had asked her more than once. The farthest he had gotten was an indulgent smile from her and the questionable pleasure of her saying his name once...and then having her revert back to her usual mode of address.

"Stop it. Stop playing." He had to fight to keep the rage out of his voice. The piano...it did something to him, something that all the coldheadedness he displayed in corporate settings could do nothing for.

"The terms of our agreement are quite clear, Mr Grant. You will let me use the piano for as long as I let you use me." She put it baldly and bluntly. Were this a contract negotiation he would be amused and impressed, but this was the bedroom, not the boardroom, and he didn't appreciate her glib answer in the least.

"Just stop playing that damnable instrument." He walked towards her, intending to seize her by the shoulders, but stopped himself at the last minute. Violence would do not good. He turned away abruptly and spoke to the air.

"A man of my means could have you seized easily enough, Rachel. You could be programmed to serve me. This...agency of yours would be able to do nothing." He wasn't sure how empty a threat he was making, but it never hurt to bluff when you at least had some cards worth playing.

"You could try, Mr Grant." She turned to face him, her expression blank as usual. He suddenly realized that she would be a terror at his job, with expressions that no one could read or fathom. "You do not presently have any rights to seize me or order to me do anything beyond what our agreement has stipulated." Not to mention a keen legal sense.

She was right, but he would be damned if he would admit it. "Get out." His voice was low, guttural, even beast-like. It came from somewhere deep inside that he had never known existed. All his desire and need had vanished in the face of what was welling up inside of him.

She played a few last notes as if taunting him, then stood and dressed with her customary inhuman grace. He turned to face her as she was leaving, and as their eyes met...was there just the faintest hint of a smile on those rouged lips?

A few seconds later the door hissed and she was gone, and he was left with only the blackness and hunger within him.

★★★★★★

At first he had been angry - who was she to dictate terms? - but the agency had been oh-so-polite about everything. I'm sorry, Mr Grant, she is not available today. No, Mr Grant, we don't approve of our members "putting on airs" but each is entitled to their own rights and priviledges. Mr Grant, the subject of ownership and rentals relating to android rights is unfortunately beyond my expertise - if we could direct you to our legal department?

In the end he had given up. She didn't want to come, not if she couldn't play the piano, and that was that. He had shouted down the phone a few times and that had made him feel better... knowing he could vent all his frustration and all he would hear was the cool, clear voice at the other line telling him no, Mr Grant, and yes, Mr Grant, and we regretfully apologize for any inconvenience you might be experiencing. He was pretty sure that there was another android on the other line - probably female as well, though you could never really tell with them - and in a brief flight of fancy he debated asking for the receptionist instead.

But he didn't. It wouldn't be the same. He didn't want any other girl, now - he wanted her. And he didn't know how the agency could refuse his demands. After all, he was prepared to pay in cash, up front, and he was not a man that you wanted on your bad side. He had toyed with other ideas - blackmail, coercion - and had settled on trying to bribe the company representative they had sent down one week.

It had been of no use. The representative (not an android) had blinked his eyes once, pretended not to notice, and come right back to offering him a premium membership. Or some kind of deal in which he could possibly rent three girls for the price of one. He couldn't remember which and didn't care.

It was stupid. Getting this worked up over an android, a mere machine. And yet - it still nagged at him, teased him. He wanted her, but he couldn't have her. In a rare flight of fantasy he had even once thought of having her forcibly repossessed. Androids - no matter how sophisticated or well-made - were in the end property. They could only be owned, never own. And so if the writ of ownership was transferred from the agency to him...sure, it was illegal, but if you threw enough money at something, laws had their ways of changing.

And yet it didn't seem right somehow. Too crude, unrefined. No finesse. His father wouldn't have approved.

He scowled and took a particularly savage swig of his drink. He had taken to drinking more when Rachel was here and now even when she had gone, the habit persisted.

How had his father gotten mixed up in this? He supposed it was the music - the damned music. He had gotten better at blocking it out during the past few months, but it still bothered him. He could almost hear the tinkling of the keys in the back of his mind, and her too-white fingers dancing over the keyboard.

The old man had always liked the piano - couldn't play it, but liked it. He had never moved it out of the room, never even allowed anyone except certain staff members to touch it, even hired an expert to tune the damn thing when he knew well enough no one in the family could either play it or wanted to. The piano had class, the old man declared, class and quality.

And on rare occasions when he wasn't shouting at people, or drawing up another deal, or screaming at him, his father would sit quietly at the stool, fingers resting on the keys, not making a sound.

Strange. He hasn't thought about his father in years. Decades, even. Why should he? The old man was gone. Dead and buried. And there had been no love lost between the two of them either, just endless shouting matches and arguments. Frankly he had been glad when the old coot finally kicked the bucket - at least then he would have free rein of the corporation and never need to justify himself to anyone ever again.

That damn piano. He didn't even know why he kept it around. He should have junked it like he had disposed of all his father's other things. But something in him wouldn't allow him to, and if he HAD thrown it away...then Rachel wouldn't even give him the time of day.

Of course, he didn't even know that Rachel existed at that time. Or that he had a thing for androids. So he had kept the piano for reasons that continued to elude him even now.

★★★★★★

After a few months, he gave in. His desire for her (need, rather) overwhelmed his reason and his hatred, and one day he found himself dialling the number of the company and saying yes, he would allow her to come back to play the piano. The cool, calm voice at the other end replied in the affirmative, and they were so happy that Mr Grant had been able to reach a satisfactory agreement. He listen to the whole stream of and then slammed the phone back down onto the receiver when they were done.

An android who wanted to play the piano. This time when she came - in a green satin dress that set off the red of her hair, and an orchid in its curls - he asked her why she wanted to play the piano in the first place. He supposed that he should have asked this much earlier but for some reason it had never occurred to him.

She looked at him with that steady, blank stare that he had grown to know so well. "I like music. Especially piano music."

Why? He asked and she stared at him and replied. "Because it sounds nice."

He gave up. There was nothing you could do with answers like that. Instead of wasting more time he simply took her to bed, had his way with her, and then lay resting on it as she got up and played as usual.

He had experimented with various methods of blocking out the noise over the months that they had been together. Looking out the window, his old favorite. Thinking about anything except the music. Even going through his work schedule and what he needed to do on any given day. In the end he had found that a combination of musing and staring at the bleak grey cityscape worked the best, and so that is what he did, desperately trying to distract himself from the tinkling of the keys.

A string of high notes tore him out of his reverie. For some reason he was sensitive to the high sounds, and he had asked her on more than one occasion to not play pieces that had too many of them.

"Well, it depends on the song, really. Some of them have more than others." was her only reply. Not a yes, not a no. She would look at him for a second, expression blank - then go back to her music.

He shot her an annoyed glance, but she was oblivious to his irritation and played on, one soaring note after another. After a minute or so of that she stopped and turned to him.

"Don't you like the music?"

Like...like the music? He barely was able to tolerate it for their agreement. Rage flared through him again but strangely enough this time it passed quickly enough.

"No. I don't like the music." He answered simply.

"I see." She regarded him steadily for a moment and then slipped off the chair to get dressed. It seemed like the concert was over for today.

★★★★★★

Another week passed and found them back in the same state as before.

They were drinking again but alcohol this time. He had asked if she could metabolize the liquor and she had nodded. He supposed that it would simply be drained from her digestive systems later and reconstituted - all androids had functional digestive tracts so they could mimic the act of consumption, but since they ran on power cells, anything that they ate or drank had to be voided somehow later.

He tried not to think too much about it. It broke the illusion of their seeming humanity too brutally for him to enjoy her company.

She had looked at each drink slowly, pale eyes blinking, and then had held it up to the light so she could watch bubbles float through the amber liquid. A curious android - now he had seen everything. Then again, he had never met an android who loved piano music either.

They toasted and drank, and then her eye fell on a bottle of pills on the table. She picked it up. It was one of their products. He didn't know why he kept it in his room in the first place.

"What's this?"

He wasn't sure what she meant. "What do you mean?"

She pointed to the bottle and nodded. He caught himself staring at the nape of her neck, so very white...too white, whiter than any human neck could or had the right to be. But he managed to retain enough presence of mind to answer.

"Oh, that. It's just something we make."

She raised one perfectly manicured eyebrow. "Do you ever take it yourself?"

"No, never use my own products. Bad form."

"Maybe you should consider using them, Mr Grant. Then you might not need the services of piano-playing androids any longer." He took there, shocked, as a slight smile played around her otherwise smooth and even features.

Then, before he could formulate a reply, she was gone. Until next week, at least. He wasn't even surprised that she hadn't played the piano this time.

★★★★★★

She wore a different flower in her hair each time she came, but most of the time they were roses. He didn't know or ask how she knew he liked them - just like he didn't know or ask how. He supposed in all their time spent together she had learnt more about him that he had realized. Either that or her programmers were skilled enough at interpretative analysis to enable her to guess. Whatever the case he liked it, and so he didn't complain.

He grew to like the scent of roses. He ordered that his office be scented - just a faint odor, he didn't want to overpower his clients' noses. It was done the next day, and he thought it was a vast improvement. He even debated hanging some paintings of roses on the walls, but decided against it - it would clash with the color, and with the scent already present the effect might be too strong.

Fake roses, sir? his assistant had inquired. They might go well with the decor. On impulse he had said yes, and the next day a dozen beautifully crafted roses in a variety of colors arrived. He tried placing them on his desk, on the chairs, on the walls – but somehow they just didn't look right. He abandoned the idea and went back to just the scent.

He didn't even ask about real roses. He was aware of how much they cost. He could afford them outside in the gardens, were they had their intended effect – instilling a sense of awe in anyone who was visiting. Anything else was an extravagant expense that he couldn't justify even with the amount of money at his disposal.

She seemed to like the effect. He had no idea if androids could smell, and if so, how well – but on the day that he had the scent put in he fancied that she smiled just a little more than usual. She turned playful, almost coquettish, and teased him in and out of bed with word games and subtle gestures.

Or it could all be in his mind. It was hard to tell with androids. Still, he was happy to partake of the illusion. The cold businesslike part of his mind reasoned that it was a small cost to pay for her imagined happiness. And another, more cynical part thought the scent of fake roses for the false joy of a human fascimile...somehow appropriate.

But another part of him was just glad she liked it.

★★★★★★

She was playing the piano again, and he was trying to do his utmost to block it out. Again. He had supposed that it would get easier each time but it actually seemed to become harder. The notes would do their gentle cascade up and down and he would grit his teeth and try to think about something else and very often almost succeed.

He had finally made the connection between the piano and his anger. It was simple, really – his father. He should have seen it way before but the life he lead left little time for reflection and introspection. His world was simple – money, making more of it...that, and android girls who played the piano.

The old man had made his life a living hell, and not just through business either. Nothing was ever good enough for him - not their revenues, not the clothes that they wore, not any of his sons and daughters. He wasn't the only one who resented the old man's critical ways...his sister refused to have anything to do with him altogther, and the family as a whole had heaved a collective sigh when he has finally died.

So why hadn't he destroyed the piano? Sentimentalism, he guessed. That and the fact that it was quite an expensive instrument indeed. He could afford another if he had to but... he didn't quite understand it himself, just like he couldn't quite understand his attraction to Rachel.

He looked out the window again. Rows upon rows upon rows of smokestacks greeted his eyes. He supposed smokestacks wasn't quite the proper term. Firstly, they didn't even blow out smoke. But he had read about it in a book somewhere and it seemed the right thing to call them.

"Do you ever get bored of looking at them?" She didn't even raise her head to look at him now when she asked. He turned to answer, noting that her forehead was creased as she navigated a particularly complex sequence of notes. In that brief second she was more radiant than ever. Not that he would ever tell her that.

"No." Somewhere along the way he had gotten into her habit of giving short, simple answers.

She played on for a while and left him to his thoughts. And then came another question.

"Do you often think about the people in the buildings, Mr Grant?" My, she was inquisitive today. He supposed that he had better humor her.

"No, not really. I don't need to know anything about them except the fact that they buy from me."

"And what is it that you sell?"

"You don't know?" He paused and looked at her, uncertain and incredulous. She looked back with wide, honest eyes, then nodded, indicating with that simple motion that yes, she didn't know, and yes, she would like to. "You really don't...well, we sell Priespex."

"And what is that?"

"Priespex. For when you're feeling alone." He rattled off the product line glibly, smiling a little at himself. "I wouldn't think androids need things like that, though."

"I suppose not. Humans might, though." She paused. "And those are in those bottles of yours?

He nodded yes and asked a question of his own. "And if you were human?"

She laughed, raising a hand to her mouth. "I didn't think of that. After all, I'm not." Then she turned to him, eyes suddenly filled with impish glee. "And you? What if you were an android? Perhaps then you would like piano music."

"But I'm not. And I don't." he said shortly.

"I guess not." she replied. After a moment's pause she returned to her piano playing.

★★★★★★

On her next visit he asked to go out to dinner with her and she accepted.

He supposed that this was what they called a date. He had selected one of the finest restaurants in the city - money was no expense, not to him - and they had driven there in the same car he took to work everyday. He had had his assistants pick out a suit for him - something subdued, nothing too fancy. Then he had even gotten a bottle of wine. Alcoholic, of course.

This was more deviant behavior than even his dalliances with her. He was treating her like a human being. And why wouldn't he? Android or no, she was more real to him than anyone he had ever known or met.

Unlike everyone else he knew she was unafraid to voice her opinions or viewpoints. From her there would be no trite replies or rehearsed speeches. Even the sudden stop-start of her eyelids as she blinked was more concrete than the drone of corporate wageslaves that he had to listen to every day.

So they had gone on their date, and it was the most pleasant evening he could remember in recent memory. The food was excellent, and the company even more so. There was soft music to accompany their meal, and somewhere in the middle of it he had watched in something approaching rapture as she had lifted a finger to dab at a stray trickle of juice running down her cheek.

Once he had even made a feeble attempt at a joke and she had laughed - whether at his delivery or effort he couldn't know.

And afterwards they had gone back to his rooms and made love with a gentleness and intensity that astounded him. He wondered for a moment whether she was happy. Could androids feel? Was it all just algorithim and analysis, endless rounds of computation in data banks and internal storage? Did they sleep, or dream...and if they did indeed do the latter, what did they dream of? Electric sheep, or roses and pianos?

He had learned to stop asking questions when it came to her, not in the least because they would never be answered. And as she traced a hand langourously across his naked chest as they lay cooling, he reflected on the fact that he didn't need to know.

★★★★★★

And then one day she disappeared. Just like that.

Their customary meeting was supposed to take place but instead there was no contact from her. He waited one hour, then two, and then three. Nothing. Finally he called the agency but they were no help either. All he got were the familiar rehearsed replies and pat answers. They couldn't tell him where she went, or why she wasn't here in the first place. Once again, nothing.

His worry and upset soon transformed into anger, and he grew furious again. At himself? At her? Both, probably. Her for disappearing without so much as a by your leave, and himself for caring so much.

He called the agency again a week later but predictably they gave no reply or forwarding address. Ever professional, they suggested a variety of replacements. There was a new model in stock, apparently almost human-like in actions and mannerisms. The receptionist (probably an android herself) suggested delicately that she would be able to take care of needs, whatever they were.

He didn't care if they made an android who could fly or could juggle or count backwards. Nor did he care how human or robotic any replacement might be. He wanted her and nothing else. But she was nowhere to be found.

The piano sat in a corner of his room, abandoned and forgotten, and each time he looked at it he felt the twin emotions of longing and hatred well up in his heart.

Despite how pained he felt, he wasn't as badly affected as he thought he would be. The scent of roses still lingered around the room and served to blunt the loss somewhat. He didn't feel the desperate hunger of the first few weeks, when she had left because he didn't allow her to play the piano. No, what he felt now was more of a dull ache, a certain grey emptiness not unlike the color of the skies outside the city.

But he would be lying if he said he didn't miss her. He tried working more, but that didn't help. All it did was stress him out more, which in turn made him desire relief more, which led him to remember how she was so good at coaxing the cares and aches of the day from him, and how soft her lily-white body was against his.

He almost considered taking his own medicine. For when you're alone...but he wasn't alone, not really. She was always around him - inside his mind, under his skin, lingering in his thoughts and emotions.

After a month he dispensed with the smell, because it did two things to him - it drove him almost crazy with desire, and it distracted him from work. A splinter in his mind that caught between the memory of the past and the bitter reality of the present.

It was one day as he was staring out from his window - a habit he couldn't quite break - that the thought occurred to him. Real roses might work where fake ones only served to remind him of her. He had plenty of them outside his mansion, and since they weren't taken care of as well as he would like, why not do that himself? It would be a welcome change from pining after something that he couldn't have.

So he took up gardening. He had staff who could tend the gardens for him, but this time he wanted to do it himself, to see each bloom be nurtured into health and growth by his own hands. The ones he had under his employ were incompetent in any case. They could never grow roses the same shade as the ones in her hair.

It was more calming that he had ever thought it could be. The cycles of birth and death, growth and decay. A man of his position was unaccustomed to having to wait for anything - besides her, of course - and now he was forced to deal with the rhythms of soil and seed, where all the money and power in the world would not make them grow any faster or better.

It was a humbling experience which gave him ample time for self-reflection. Amidst cutting, shearing and pruning of rosebushes, he mused to himself that he would never have thought that he would enjoy working with his hands so much. But then again he never would have thought that he would come to be so attached to an android either. Or that she would leave.

His days and weeks became punctuated by the blooming and dying of roses. Before it was her visits, but now each round of death and rebirth was how he kept time. They grew, they died and then their petals fell. There was a tranquil regularity about it that he grew to relish and enjoy.

But ever so often he still dreamt of her, and his body would ache with suppresse desire. He longed to see her - to touch her – again, and the roses could only do so much. But for now, that were all that he had.

★★★★★★

The roses were blooming well this week.

He touched one gently, feeling the spring and resilience in the petals even as his fingertips registered their softness.

As his skills had progressed he had tried to plant more and more, experimenting with different blooms over time. Blue roses were the hardest. They never seemed to want to grow, fragile and recalcitrant and drooping at the slightest touch. Then he tried the yellow, which were a little better. They took to the soil easily enough but they still seemed to wilt without constant attention.

He went with others as well. Purple, hardy but prone to mold. White, difficult to grow at first but well worth the effort it took. Blue, vivid and arresting.

But he always came back to the red roses. They were robust, strong and managed to grow in whatever conditions he put them in. When meetings prevented him from coming to the gardens as often as he liked, they weathered his absence without shedding a single petal.

He couldn't lie to himself any more – he had planted the roses because they reminded him of her. The hue of carmine called to the mind the shade of her lips and most of all, the flower in her hair that she had had in it when they first met.

He plucked the one that he was holding onto and moved on to the next.

Roses. How his life seemed to have become filled with them. From memories of her to the gardens that he worked on almost everyday now. As time passed he had gotten better at cultivating them and soon he had so many of them that he didn't know what to do. He ended up putting them in vases, one in his room and the rest in his office.

Some clients even commented on how nice they looked, but he didn't care what they thought. He hadn't brought them in for them. He did like the way they looked, though. Also, they didn't smell very strongly and he was actually very glad of that.

He had almost ordered the piano destroyed as well, but at the last minute he had changed his mind. It reminded him of his father, yes – which is why he had so hated her playing it all this time – but it also reminded him of her, and how she would sit naked after their lovemaking, her long white fingers dancing rapidly over the keys where only minutes before they had dragged climax after climax from his gasping body.

He had even considered learning to play it once...but no. The roses were enough for him.

It was one day in the gardens when he was weeding and pruning that it came - a call. He had told his office to hold all calls for the week. He had just finished a particularly tricky contract negotiation with Paradyne Corporation, and he needed time for himself after three gruelling days spent doing nothing but crunching numbers and discussing figures.

Wait. There was only one person who had this number. He put down the shears and put the phone that was never far from him to his ear.

"Richard. I wanted to see you." It was her. He would know that voice anywhere – half girl, half woman. Soft, but with just a hint of breathiness to it. The same voice that had whispered to him in bed and giggled in amusement while they were talking.

"Where have you been?" He tried and failed to keep the trembling out of his voice.

"I won't be able to see you anymore. I just wanted you to know that...to know that..." – was that indecision in heard in her tone? Or something else? She continued before he could be sure.

"I enjoyed our time together, and I will be sad to leave. Keep the piano in tune for me, won't you?"

He knew better than to plead, or to ask her to reconsider. He could try tracing the call but he had a suspicion that wouldn't work either. The agency would be of no use. In the end she would do whatever she wanted to do, because that was who she was.

He was still standing there thinking of what to say when the line went dead abruptly.

He stood there for a few moments, unmoving, then placed the receiver back onto the handset gently. Then he went up to his rooms.

And there he took the vase of roses that was in it, put it on top of the piano, and left.

★★★★★★

Dark Knight

THEY CAME.

From countless gates, out of the void, swarming, crawling, slithering. In all forms and guises, many-legged or none, the hordes came.

But he was there to stop them. No matter how many arrived, no matter what shape they took or how many appeared at once, he was there to beat them back. To stem the tide and halt their advance, and then finally to shut whichever gate they had come from.

Who were they? Where had they come from? Those questions had long since ceased to matter. They could not be allowed to reach her. She who slept at the heart of all things. They would come, but he would stop them. That was all that he knew, all that existed in the world.

Each day - if days existed here, seemingly beyond time and space - he would patrol the gates. Check his weapons, clean them, and sharpen any that needed his attention. Then he would make his rounds, passing by each marble portal, watching, waiting. Sometimes nothing appeared, and then he would return to train, and practice, and sharpen his weapons some more. To wash in one of the many fountains and to pray. Pray for the strength and fortitude to defend this place against whatever came, for the grace of she who still slept.

Then returning to watch, and to wait. Again and again. He had long stopped counting - if he had ever started. Time had no meaning here. Only the waiting, and the inevitable battles that would come.

And after watching, and after waiting, they would indeed come. Then battle would be joined.

★★★★★★

Try as he might, he could never remember the battles clearly. One minute it was quiet, and then next hordes of shadow would stream from the gates.

As he was taught, he abandoned all thought, all cognition. Moving at one with his weapons, he became a whirlwind of destruction - hacking, slashing, chopping, hewing in all directions. There was no room for thought, no time for decisions. Only motion and action, remained.

He fought with no regard for his own safety, with no sense of time, simply moving, surviving. From one second to the next. Become the blade, become the enemy. Abandon the self, embrace the storm of war.

And when the flow of shadow had abated, when he became conscious that nothing moved around him save himself, he would open his eyes, come back to where he stood, and see that the gates had closed once more, and that the fight was over. That she was safe.

Then time for prayer. To rejoice in what time he had been given before the next assault. To train and practice and wait until the cycle began anew. What waited at the end - if there was an end - he knew not. It was not given to him to know, and to tell the truth he never even conceived of it. He was to guard the gates, and that was all that existed for him.

It was enough.

★★★★★★

Still, there were times when it was different. Without truly being conscious of it, he would see the sky reflected in a pool. The play of light on marble would catch his eye, and he would turn, and it would be gone when he dared to look directly at it. He would hear sounds, music, almost - a hint of a faraway melody. Birdsong, perhaps.

He paid them no heed. They were nothing, just distractions. He was here to guard the gates, and protect her. That was all he was, all he needed, all he remembered.

But even so, from time to time, he caught himself wondering. He cast his eye around where he walked and it suddenly dawned on him how beautiful everything was - from the bright pools of water to the shimmer of light all around. From the inlaid marble of the gates to the carvings on the walls.

Did it matter that he thought them beautiful? He still had a mission to carry out. Nothing had changed. But slowly but surely the knowledge of something besides battle began to dawn in his heart, without him quite realizing where and when it had happened, or for what reason.

He bent to clean his weapons once more, so they would be sharp and ready for the next battle, and all thoughts of beauty went from his mind. One purpose, as always - to protect her, and to kill her that would seek to harm her. That was all that consumed him and ever would.

★★★★★★

Battle gave way to battle after battle and as time passed he suddenly realized one day that he had never even seen her and didn't even know her name. Why was he even here? Why did he have to protect her? He didn't know, but it didn't make his task any less compelling.

Still, as a thousand more shadows fell to his blade he began to wonder. What she really looked like. Where was she? Beyond those gates that he had stood in front of a hundred times before? Somewhere deeper?

Why was he doing this? To protect her, of course. But why do that? Because he loved her? Because...he didn't know.

He realized that he didn't really know anything. He looked down at his sword and saw his reflection, but it was of somebody whom he had no knowledge or recollection of. He turned to the fountains, and the marble, and everything that he thought he knew so well but now were revealed as more mysteries, more illusions.

He found himself contemplating blasphemy...opening the gates by himself and stepping inside. He felt a fierce rage at himself for even thinking of it. How could he? He was her guardian. He could no sooner open the gates than invite the shadows themselves inside.

Or that was what he told himself, but as each day passed he found himself thinking of what lay within more and more. The thought consumed him from the inside out and wouldn't leave - what did she look like? Who was she?

Why was he even here?

More shadows came and more shadows fell, and in the dimmest part of his mind a memory began to form.

★★★★★★

They were dancing in a garden somewhere, a long long time ago. He knew what she looked like - long white hair, gentle blue eyes, laughter and smiles to gladden the heart of anyone. He took her hand and she took his and they spun and twirled together in perfect harmony.

He was...a prince? A nobleman. He couldn't quite remember. He looked so strange in those clothes...high collar, open jacket and tailored pants. So different from the armor that he had always found himself in. But they were open and loose and free and so it was easy- so easy, for him to keep dancing.

She danced beside him in the garden, bright and carefree, hands linked. They spun and broke in unison and came together again, and then broke away again, as if it was the most natural thing in the world.

The memory faded as quickly as it had come, in a bright flash of light, and he was back at in the present.

★★★★★★

Another battle passed and before he knew it he was in front of the gates. The garden, and the dance, swirled through his mind in much the same way they had spun and twirled so long ago. Lost in reverie, his grip on the sword began to loosen.

It happened without him thinking about it. His hand was upon the handle and he had turned it without even realizing that he had even made the motion. He gasped in shock but it was too late - the gates had been opened. And by his own hand no less.

They opened and then...nothing. There was nothing within. A wide open expanse of bare stone and nothing else. Only an opened coffin, resting in the middle.

He stepped inside, his hands tracing the marble inlay on the gates that was so similar to the ones outside. What had he expected would be waiting for him here? His princess? The truth? Anything but this.

Maybe she was inside. He took a step forwards, then another, and another. Hope warred with worry and fought with trepidation, only to be defeated by anticipation. One, two, three...and he was there, staring at the empty space in front of him.

No one. Nothing except a single velvet pillow.

He began to tremble, not in fear but with something far more terrible. Had he slain all those shadows for nothing? Where was she? Who was she? He clutched at his sword again and thought that he might go mad. He could have been prepared for anything except this...this emptiness.

But then from deeper within came a voice - high and singsong, bright laughter that brought a vision of faraway and long ago. His feet moved of their own volition and he began to walk further within.

★★★★★★

The frescoes that adorned the walls were somehow familiar, somehow nostalgic and sentimental. He had seen them before, he was sure of that. Where, he could not be certain, but somewhere, definitely. The shapes and images - like the marble inlay of the gates, but not really the same either.

He continued walking. He walked for so long that he began to doubt if he had ever heard that voice after all, the lilting tones that had brought him past the gates and further on. But they were real, and he was sure that he had heard them, and so he continued onwards, one foot on front of the other.

Eventually he came to another set of gates. They had a different marble inlay, and they were white instead of black. He wasted no time in putting hand on handle and those gates opened as well, and the light spilled forth, and then -

He was here. In the garden that he had danced with her in another reality...or was it simply many years before? Was it even him?

Who was he? Prince or knight or both? The same questions swam in his head and he stepped forwards, wondering.

She stood at the center of the garden, bright light playing off her crown of hair of snowy hair. She turned smiling, and everything fell from him - all weariness, questions and confusion. She was there and that was all that mattered.

"Thank you, my knight. I've been waiting." Waiting for what? For him to have killed enough shadows? For him to have opened the gates? He opened his mouth to speak but found that he couldn't.

"I knew that you would grow tired one day, and come back to me."

He didn't understand. What was happening? Why all that battle and strife, then? Was it useless? Had he wielded his sword so long and so truly only for it all to before naught?

She came closer to him and took his hand. She touched her lips to his, and he remembered.

★★★★★★

It was the curse. All of her lineage had it and she was no exception. Left unchecked it would destroy the kingdom and everything they held dear. The oracles had divined it truly, as they had every single one before - she had to be killed. There was no other way

Where had it come from? No one knew. Some say that it was born of the shadow that had existed before the land even came to take shape.

He could not believe it, could not accept it. Finally he found one.

They made the pact in the garden. Where they had danced and spun so many times on many a moonlit night. He drew his blade and she closed her eyes and where their hands touched the shadow passed from her into him.

One day the memory of her would be stronger than what he faced, and then he would be able to put down his sword and return to the garden where once they had danced together. Until then he would have to fight, blinded by oblivion and ignorance, against foes that were not even his. Shadow upon shadow would come and he would slay them all, not knowing that they came from him.

It was a burden he accepted willingly. It was no small price to be able to see her again, when it was all over. Their eyes met and she smiled a halting smile. He tried to return it but he could not.

He took up the sword and the darkness claimed him. Everything passed from his vision - the kingdom, the garden, her worried face as she looked at him. Only darkness remained.

He would know nothing else for a thousand years.

★★★★★★

But now...now it was all over, and looking at her radiant face he felt that he could have endured for a thousand more, if it meant coming to this point. To hold her hands in his and feel the warmth of her skin once more. He was her knight - sworn to protect - and he had done that for a long time indeed.

"Come here, my love. Receive your reward."

He knelt, eyes closed, head bowed. She came to him and her arms encircled his, feather-light and gentle. The kiss was a benediction on the crown of his head.

His true reward? Her safety. His return. The shadows had come and gone and he was home again once more. Tears fell from his eyes and she met each with another kiss. Her hand touched his face and pulled it to her. She looked deep into his eyes and smiled again.

They danced in each other's eyes for what seemed an eternity or longer. Here in this space beyond light and shadow, they knew nothing except each other. His sword fell from his side and her hand dropped down to find his. The curse was broken and the lovers had found each other once more.

Slowly - ever so slowly - she raised her arms in an oh-so familiar position. He found himself smiling this time as his body shifted into patterns that he had thought long gone.One step, then another, and they were dancing once more, entwined in each other's arms. A thousand years had not dulled the memory of light one bit.

Moment blended into movement and as they spun and whirled as they had many times before, it seemed like all past and darkness unraveled and was lost.

And they lived happily ever after.

The Fisherman

FLIP, CATCH, RELEASE. A hit.

Reel it in, take it off the hook.

He took aim again, making sure the fish was in his sights. He almost never missed, but it always paid to be careful.

Flip, catch, release.

That was his day, and much of his night as well. If he didn't fish, he would starve. There was not much else to do here, or think of, besides survival.

The waves grew unbroken on the shoreline, and he righted the boat slightly, making sure that none of the water spilled in. It would be dangerous if it did.

He had to be sure of each cast. He squinted slightly, making sure that his target was lined up clearly. There, he had it.

Flip, catch, release.

★★★★★★

The past few days had been full of bad weather, and his stocks were running low. He had spent most of the time making sure the capacitor and rudder were in working condition.

If they failed, he couldn't sail. If he couldn't sail he couldn't fish and if that happened he would die. So it made sense to maintain them as well as possible.

His stock of sonic disruptors was being steadily depleted, and there was a limit to how many he could scavenge. They were good for catching a lot of fish at once - just throw it into the water and watch them all be stunned by the emissions, and then sweep them up with the net afterwards. But they would run out. It was just him and his harpoon now.

At times like this he thought of going back to shore, to civilization. But something always stopped him. The people there couldn't be trusted. They would lie, cheat and steal from you without so much as a second thought. If he wanted to sell five fishes he knew someone would sneak behind him and take ten. Ask them for anything and they sneered and shook their heads. He was better off without humanity, of that he was sure.

He would do the best he could out here, or die trying. It was just like in the war, except that this time it was him against the waves, instead of against the 'bots. Nothing much had changed. Harpoon instead of gun, boat instead of ship. Still a battle for survival, just like it always was.

In an hour he was out on the boat again and fishing as usual. The waves grew high and fast, but he simply adjusted for that. The maintenance work had paid off, and his control was better than it had ever been.

Flip, catch, release. Cast once and re-sight, and then cast again. Nothing to it. The same thing day after day.

He wiped the sweat from his brow and took aim again.

Flip, catch, release.

★★★★★★

He never really liked the taste of the fish he caught. Too much oil, even after the refinement process. His teeth would slip away from the slick flesh and he would have to make sure he didn't end up biting himself.

But it was still an improvement from army rations. He remembered the days when they had to open up cans of stinking food after a march. The officers insisted it was nutritious –and it very well could have been - but Anything was better than that.

He couldn't complain. He was still alive. He had fish to eat. It could be worse.

Sometimes, he remembered things. His life before the war, before the 'bots came. Army barracks and friends and stories shared around an open campfire. Green fields and open skies. But they were all distant memories, belonging to another world and another time, so far removed from the oily water and the fish and the boat that they may as well have been the recollections of someone else. Which they were, in a way.

He stood up. Thinking wouldn't feed him. He took hold of the harpoon again and sighted it.

Flip, catch, release.

★★★★★★

It was the next day he saw her.

He had suspected that something was unusual before he had even started the day. It was something in the waves, in the water. He didn't know what it was exactly but he had spent enough time out on the open ocean to be able to read the tides to some degree. It bothered him for a while, but then he stopped thinking about it. There was no point trying to find out what you couldn't.

But then she appeared. First a silver fin broke the shimmering surface of the water, and then a slim shoulder, and then he saw her

He looked, but she was gone as fast as she had appeared. At first he thought that he was merely seeing an illusion, a hologram cast by one of the undersea vessels that even now - but no, the ripples in the water that she left were real. She was there one second and then gone the next.

★★★★★★

He saw her again the next day.

She broke the water near to him, swimming first fast then slow, turning one way and then another. He saw her flukes shimmer in the sunlight and had to incline his head away from their blinding reflection.

"Hello." Her voice was high, almost musical.

He paid no attention. He had another catch in his sights. She could wait. Steady now.

Flip, catch, re - "Hey, I said hello!"

He missed. It was the first time he had missed in more than a hundred throws. He turned to look at her.

He could see her properly for the first time. Long black hair, eyes of silver-grey, and a face that before the war he might have called beautiful. She stared at him, treading water, an unreadable expression on her face. She turned away suddenly.

"You want fish? Fine."

She turned and sang.

A blast of pure sound ripped through the water next to him. It was far stronger than any sonic disruptor, a focused blast of fluid that sprayed and shot in all directions,

There were indeed plenty of fish floating in the wake of the eruption, enough for a week at least. He stood there for a while, struck dumb.

When he came to his senses she had disappeared. He couldn't tell if she was angry or upset or both. He wasn't even sure what she was. This far out on the water, there should only have been the fish, the waves and maybe the odd patrol drone that had gone missing. She was none of those things.

He shrugged. It was no using wondering. Wondering didn't feed you. He hefted the harpoon again and went back to work.

★★★★★★

She did not appear for the next week, or the next.

Despite himself his thoughts came back to her again and again. He was not sure what to make of her. He had encountered nothing similar in the war. Was she a cyborg? Most probably. There was no surviving in these waters without some kind of augmentation. She looked too human, too alive to be a robot, and he couldn't think of anyone or anything advanced enough to construct an android that could both swim and project sonic blasts.

He spent a few more minutes wondering before shaking himself out of it. The waves were getting rougher and he had to make sure that he brought in at least three more catches before the day was out.

In the end things remained the same. It didn't quite matter who she was or what he thought of her. He still had to eat. There were still fish to catch.

Flip, catch, release.

★★★★★★

The skies were overcast for the next few days. It was dangerous to go out in such weather, and so he stayed in the small cabin near the rocks which he called home. There was always maintenance work to be done, and if there wasn't, he could always go to the shore and just sit and watch the waves. It calmed him to be able to do that – he didn't quite know why.

On day when he was doing just that, out of the corner of his eye he thought he saw a fin splash and go by, but it could just have been a trick of the light. Reflections on oil had a way of playing with your eyes, making you think something was there when it was not. You had to be careful. He had lost more than one fish that way.

Eventually the weather cleared and he set out on his boat once more.

Flip, catch, release. Another day on the ocean.

★★★★★★

The squid appeared out of nowhere. One moment the ocean was calm and steady, and the next he could see a shapeless grey mass rushing beneath the oily water. He could barely make out tentacle after tentacle unwrapping themselves from the main bulk of the

He cursed his carelessness. He should have checked. He should have known that after inclement weather one of them might appear - relics of the war, designed for crippling enemy ships but now just aimlessly destroying anything they came into contact with. He should have been more alert, shouldn't have gone so far into deep water.

But it was too late for regrets. He leaned back to supercharge the capacitor so he could get away faster...or maybe he should try to fight, try to distract the thing with his harpoon? He was about to decide when a stray tentacle lashed out at him from the boat's side.

Just as suddenly, she appeared to the side as well. Before he could do anything she had already opened her mouth to sing. The same blast of sound echoed forth from her, splitting the water and striking the squid head-on. It recoiled in shock and she sang again, another keen note which

The squid thrashed about for a while, and then with a high-pitched whine its servos activated and it shot towards them, tentacles thrashing wildly.

He couldn't tell if it had been hunting her or if his fishing had attracted it, but it was not the time to think about that. He threw the harpoon long and high, and had the satisfaction of seeing it slam deep into the squid's rubbery hide. It didn't stop but it slowed, long enough for him to pull back the weapon for another throw.

But then another tentacle was snaking towards him. If he got to his spare, he could - but it was too fast, so if he -

Her scream cut off his train of thought. It was even more powerful than her previous song, a channel of sound that he could almost see that cut cleanly through the squid's appendages. One, two - no, even more. She kept it up, the sound slicing through tentacle after tentacle before finally opening a hole in the main body of the squid itself.

"Wait!" he was about to cry. But with a swish of her tail she was gone.

★★★★★★

Days passed.

He found himself hoping that he would see her again. Hoping didn't feed you, he knew, but he hoped nonetheless.

The seas seemed different somehow. Restless. Maybe it was just how he felt, but he thought that the waters seemed rougher, choppier. He was used to the sea's moods by now – at times calm, sometimes steady, and often wild, but this wasn't the same.

Why did she matter to him now, when she didn't before? Because they fought the squid together? Because she had saved him, or him her?

He wasn't used to asking and answering questions like that. He was a man of the sea, and before that, a man of war. To him, life was simple. Kill or be killed, eat or be eaten. He obeyed laws that had existed ages before the earth was cool, before the wars had been fought, before the technology that had turned the sea into oil and its creatures into metal was even invented. Simple laws, primordial and eternal.

Was it those same laws that gave rise to his sudden yearning? He shook his head. Too many questions.

He took up his harpoon again, sighted, and threw.

Flip, catch, release.

★★★★★★

A week later. Still no sign of her.

He gave up hoping, or wondering, or thinking. Ever practical, he turned his mind back to fishing and his tools. Only three sonic disruptors left. Capacitor would have to be changed soon. The rudder needed fixing again. He might even need to go back to - no, not that. He would make do on his own. He could scavenge enough, he was sure.

He couldn't eat any of the squid, but he was able to salvage some servos from it which he could possibly use as spare parts. There was that, at least.

He wondered what power source she ran on. Did she need to eat? Surely she didn't eat the same fish that he ate. Maybe deeper down where she could swim there were other fish, other things within the deep sea that she could live on. Could it be solar power? But that was something the scientists were only working on before the war had started...he didn't even know of anything back in his unit that even utilized solar power - once again, there was no way to tell.

He went back to sea, and the hours grew into days which grew into weeks and then after a while it was like he had never even seen her before. Things settled back into a familiar rhythm. Maintain the boat. Sail into shallow water. Fish as many fish as he could. Keep surviving.

Flip, catch, release. But it didn't seem enough now, somehow.

★★★★★★

Another day on the water. Flip, catch, release. And then -

"Hello." He turned to see her at his side, treading water effortlessly again.

"Where have you been?" The words were out of his mouth before he could think.

She smiled. "Somewhere."

"Where did you go? I haven't seen you for weeks."

"You're talkative today."

He grew quiet. He had spoken more in those few minutes that he had in years. She seemed to know that and stopped speaking. He sent the boat out further and she followed wordlessly.

Together, they sailed on for a while. She stopped here and there to dive for...her food, maybe, whatever it was. He didn't ask and she didn't tell.

He envied her grace in the water. His boat seemed so clunky, slow and unwieldy compared to her fluid movements. But then again, she was clearly designed for the sea, her flukes and tail cutting through the murky surface cleanly and easily.

She swam around his boat once, and then dove, then came out seconds later, tossing her hair back with a laugh. Another round, another dive.

"Do you eat the fish?" He found himself asking, after she broke the surface for the third time.

"No." She looked at him and shook her head.

"What do you eat, then?"

She looked at him strangely, head cocked to the side. "Why do you want to know?"

He didn't answer. He couldn't - he didn't even know why he asked. So he simply stared at her.

"I'll be seeing you." She swung her hair carelessly and disappeared under the waves. He found himself wondering how and why the oil slid off it so easily. Then he shook his head again. Back to fishing.

★★★★★★

There was much he didn't know about her. Where she came from. What she ate. Who she was. What she was.

From that day on she appeared to talk to him every day. Sometimes in the morning, when the sun's rays made the glistening water shine brightly, sometimes in the afternoon, where the waves grew slow and calm. Almost never in the evening. He didn't ask her why.

She always talked more than him. Not a hard thing to do, considering that he rarely spoke, if at all. She told him about how far the sea stretched on – farther than he knew. About how many squid there actually were in the deepest parts of the ocean. Where there fish went when they weren't near the surface.

He listened quietly and never said anything. He was learning more about the world in which he lived everyday than he had ever imagined, but still he set out on his boat each day to fish, to bring his catch back to be refined and then to eat it. It was still about survival, but now there was something else. The mermaid and her stories.

One day she began to ask him questions about the war. At first he didn't want to speak about it at all, but there was something in her voice that made him start to hesitantly talk about it. The long marches from base to base. The lasers from assault carriers above which split the sky and burnt base after base to ash. The 'bots swarming one after another, how they would cut down a hundred only to have a thousand appear.

"Why do you want to know?" he asked her back one day. He couldn't understand why she would want to know about the war. She had obviously been created after it.

"No reason." She shook her head, sending oil drops flying.

He left it at that, content to continue fishing with her by his side. She never fished for him by singing again, and he was glad of it. It meant that he could be with her longer.

★★★★★★

Weeks passed.

They fell into a steady rhythm. He would go out to sea, and at a certain point in the day she would join him. He would fish, and she would talk to him while he sighted and cast. Then she

88

would ask a single question, and he would answer, and then she would disappear swiftly into the water.

Then one day, he asked her to sing.

Silver-grey eyes looked at him quizzically. "To get fish? But you already come out here to do that."

He didn't know how to put it. He just knew that he wanted to hear her voice. Not the deadly blast of sound that killed, but another kind, meant for another purpose. But he didn't say any of that. He wasn't sure of what he meant himself.

She closed her eyes and nodded. "Alright." She opened her mouth and sang and the world changed.

It was eerie, haunting and beautiful, an ululation both pure and distorted at the same time. It reminded him of the past, of things long since forgotten, things that had existed before the war and feelings and emotions he had thought gone. Images swam in front of him - family, children (whose? his?) comrades cut down like so much fallen wheat (what was wheat? A kind of grass? grass...that grew on land?) and words he had lost the meaning of mixed together in a whirlpool of thought and memory.

He saw the sea, but this time it was blue instead of brown. He saw the sky and it was white instead of cast-iron grey. He saw...he couldn't even begin to name the things that he saw.

And then it was over. He found himself staring at the water as it rippled, lost in thought. He wasn't sure what he thought or felt. The song...the song had opened him up somehow, to things both new and old. He wasn't the same person that he was before he had heard it.

He turned to face her, but a wave swept over her and turning, she was gone.

★★★★★★

It was a while since she sang for him until she appeared again. He didn't worry because he knew she would come back.

They fell into the same patterns as before. Fish, talk, ask and then leave. But one day there were no more things to talk about or questions to be asked or answered.

But she still came every day, though, and they spent time together in much the same way as before. He sighted and cast – catch, flip and release – and she swam circles around the boat, appearing on its left and then its right, smiling at him as she glided through the water.

One day she asked him. "Are you happy here?"

"What do you mean?"

"You seem...lonely. Even with me around. Wouldn't you like to go where" she gestured to the horizon, where the ports lay "they are?"

"I'm not their kind." And he wasn't.

"But you are. You're not like me." She pirouetted in the water, showing her flukes. Yes, he didn't know what she was, but he was not like her, that was certain.

He suddenly realized that if he left, she would not be able to follow. Land seemed more and more distant every day. It was here he belonged, on the open sea, with his boat and the harpoon and the fishes and her.

"What's wrong?" He hadn't realized he was staring.

"Nothing." He turned back to cast again and when he looked back, she had disappeared.

★★★★★★

Then one day she wasn't there. There was nothing in the sea that told him of her departure. The tides had been different when she appeared, but this time there was no sign to mark her absence.

Nothing had changed. Everything had changed.

He went out to sea as usual. He still had to survive, still had to fish and to eat his catch. But she wasn't there.

A hole had opened up inside of him; a void to a space that he didn't even know existed. He felt hollow, lost...alone. It had been the song. He was sure of it. It had changed him in ways that he couldn't even begin to know. He remembered her singing, eyes closed and head raised, and thought of the sky and the sea and her.

The waves lapped insistently against the side of the boat and he shook his head. Thinking didn't feed you. It didn't do much of anything. He hefted his harpoon again.

Something welled up inside him but he put it away.

Flip, catch, release.

★★★★★★

The next week she was back.

He yearned to ask where she had gone but he didn't. She didn't say anything and simply swam up to the side of his boat, peering at him intently. He said nothing and continued fishing as usual.

"You're different." she said.

He was. He had noticed it himself. But he didn't know how to reply, and so he didn't. For a while there was silence on the open sea, only broken by the lapping of the waves and the splash of his harpoon as it hit the water.

She began to make a round past his boat as usual but suddenly tilted to her side, letting the waves carry her. She began to hum wordlessly...not a song, but not speaking either. For a while things continued in this vein - she floated on the surface and he sighted and cast again and again.

Then without warning she laughed, a high, strong note that sang out across the open ocean. He started in surprise and before he knew it she was so close to him that he could almost touch her.

"You're strange." she said. She pushed off the boat and fell back into the water, treading it lightly as she looked at him. "Not like the others at all."

What others, he wanted to ask. Have you spoken to other humans? What were they like? Where did you talk to them, when you can't go to the shore? But as usual he didn't say anything. After so many years at sea speaking was still largely unknown to him.

She smiled, closed her eyes, and dove. He was left standing there, looking at where the waves marked her passing.

★★★★★★

She was gone for a few days but this time he didn't worry. He knew she would be back...how, he wasn't sure, but he knew all the same. And so when her head broke the waters near to him he didn't even react and simply sighted and cast again. Flip, catch, release.

How much time passed he didn't know.

"I have to go now." she said simply.

"Where?" He wasn't aware that there was somewhere to go to. There was the land, of course, but she couldn't go there. And the sea...which meant somewhere else on the water, far away even beyond the deep waters where he had never dared to go.

"My sisters are waiting for me." Sisters? There was more than one of her?

Questions swam through his head and he felt like he too was a fish, caught in a sea of confusion and

"Can I go with you? When will you come back?" He couldn't believe what he was asking.

She looked and him and gave a single sad shake of her head. Then she threw it back and sang.

It wasn't the same song from before. This was a cry of such unearthly beauty that he fell back in shock, almost hitting his head on the boat's stern.

He saw blue skies and bombs, flaming wreckage and people crying out in pain. Machines that he couldn't name - not the 'bots that he had nightmares about - things far worse. Beams of light that tore through smoke and flame. The earth split open and broken apart.

He saw other things as well. Towns and cities, prosperous and bustling. Children and youths on flying vehicles that flitted easily from one place to another. Men bent over computer displays, reading letters that he found vaguely familiar. And green...so much brilliant green all around them, in trees, bushes, and leaves. It was like the war had never happened.

When he came out of the haze of memory, she was gone.

★★★★★★

Flip, catch, release. A hit.

Reel it in, take it off the hook.

The skies had been clear lately, and his dreams (he had begun to dream again) were filled with things that he couldn't even begin to name or know. Some were from before the war, some came from the songs that she had sung. He didn't know which was which anymore.

But in front of him stretched the same russet expanse of ocean that he knew so well. There were fish to be fished and boats and tools to be maintained. That was his life, much as it had always been.

He sighed and took up the harpoon again. Where had she gone? Would she ever come back? He knew deep inside - in a place deeper than even beyond the waters where her sisters waited - that he would never know the answer to those questions.

He sighted and cast. Flip, catch, release.

His eyes were drawn to the horizon, to dry land and where the rest of his people were...except that they weren't his people. Were they? Where did he belong? Here, on the open waters? Where she was...but she would never come back. Where should he go? Here. Anywhere but here.

He reeled in his catch and found himself looking up at the sky. A glimpse of white shone out among the grey. Had it been here all the time? Maybe he had simply never noticed it before.

Thinking didn't feed you, hoping didn't either. But he needed more than food, now.

He reached back to touch the capacitor and adjust the rudder. He remembered her song, and images swam before him once again. A blue sky. Green fields. And her, a sleek shape among the waves, laughing, singing, looking at him.

The boat cut out over the open sea, the man at its prow. His brow was furrowed in thought and as he made his way out along the ocean, he allowed himself to, for once in his life, not know where he was going.

Moonlit Dreams

FOR AS LONG as he could remember, he had wanted to fly.

He was the only one that he knew who had this dream. The other boys in the city had comparatively more mundane desires. They wanted horses, or carts, or sweet breads from the store. When asked about the future, some replied that they wanted to become teachers, or doctors. They were content to race around the city square and steal apples and swim in the nearby rivers, splashing and cavorting and generally having a good time.

No, not him. Each day after school or after his chores he would do the same thing – go out and walk in the grassy fields around his house, staring at the sky. Or he would climb the hill further away from the town, as if by getting a few feet more off the ground he could get closer to that vast blue that stretched above him.

The neighbors would sit and shake their heads whenever they saw him at his activities. The boy's addled, some would say. It's a stage, others said. And others still would look at his parents, who would look abashed and away. They didn't know what afflicted their only child either, to make him forego play and work and spend the better part of each day in what seemed like a daze, always looking up at the sky.

And what he loved best were the airplanes and airships that ever so often flew ahead. He often thought they looked like birds soared above him, high and graceful and beautiful. The airshows where they would be many of them were too far away from him to attend, but the hill afforded him a decent view of what was going on. There was never a day where he missed a show, and rarely still any time where he couldn't be found on the hill, gazing in rapt attention at the flying ships. When he got home he would tell his parents how he was going to get into one of them when he was older, or better yet, build one!

When he finished school his course was simple and certain - go to the Academy and become an engineer, or a pilot. His parents had sighed and shook their heads and wished him well. His father had wanted him to take over the farm, and his mother thought that perhaps a trade might suit him, carpenter, or shoemaker - something respectable. But they knew that nothing else but the open sky would satisfy him, and so after buying him a new suit and all the books that he needed, they bade him a fond farewell.

★★★★★★

He arrived at the academy without incident and his first year there was bliss. He applied himself to his studies with such vigor and tenacity that the teachers there stared in astonishment at this quiet, serious youth from the faraway villages that appeared to do nothing but read and write each and every day. He cared not for the girls that batted their eyelashes at him, or the parties that his fellow classmates seemed to live for. One thing and one thing only consumed him from dawn to dusk - the dream of flight.

But then the war came and everything changed. There were no more dances or parties to be had. The gay smiles of the pretty girls changed to frowns and eyes that once had sparkled in childish innocence now were squeezed tightly in pain. Where once there had been jokes and horseplay in class, now there was nothing more the drone of the teacher's voices and the scrawl of pens on paper.

What tore him apart more than anything was the change in the planes. As the months dragged on he saw the designs of his dreams change. Curving wood was replaced with harsh metal, paper and cloth with screws and rivets. Where once supple beams of oak had been bent to enable them to go ever higher, now black metal hugged the frames tightly. Speed was sacrificed for armor, beauty for brute strength.

He began to hate what he was studying. Where were the planes of his youth, the sleek-limbed contraptions that flew and whirled through the air with the grace of birds? Not here. They had been replaced by dark and heavy beasts of war. Doves and swallows had turned into eagles and falcons. His quick and eager stride to his classes had become a heavy slog through mud.

His only solace was in his own ideas and creations. He saved all his notes from the classes and as the curriculum changed and, he still spent night after night at the library, putting together. In his mind and fantasies the war had never come, and the planes that he saw were still the same ones that flew high and fast through the sky that he so adored and longed for.

Then came the letter. His father's farm was hard-pressed to make ends meet what with the war raging on. They were fast running out of money, and so he would have to come home. When the headmaster came to dismiss him, all full of meaningful advice and stern regret, he nodded and said yes politely and but secretly he hid the diagrams that he had drawn in the pockets of his best suit and in his luggage. Wars might come but they would never destroy his dreams.

It was cold, wet and raining when he boarded the horse and carriage that would take him home. Raindrops splattered all around him and he spent the entire coach trip back staring at the night sky.

★★★★★★

The war worsened. Food was rationed and then became almost impossible to find. Family treasures that had been kept for generations were taken out, sighed over, and then consigned to the black market. There was no talk of school anymore, or flying...just survival.

He went to the fields to work, spending most of his day in hard, backbreaking labor. Whatever meagre harvest the land provided was soon finished quickly. The very idea of riding in an airship seemed as far away now as the sky itself. But still after each day when the hoe and rake had been put away and the animals sent to their pasture, he would go up to the hill and look at the sky.

Deep inside he knew how impossible his dream was. Even if his family had money and even if the academy reopened, he couldn't even go back to the libraries. They had barred all passage to the capital a year ago, and even if he could...all they made in what was once the city of his dreams were flying machines of war, metal monstrosities than flew low and dropped bombs instead of soaring high among and over white clouds.

He remembered the planes of his youth – how they danced in the sky and made impossible shapes in that azure field that spread overhead. He bent to his work, weeding the fields with such tenacity that his parents were amazed much as the teachers in the city had been. But little did they know how much pain there was in his heart, and how it never seemed to lessen despite how much he tilled the soil and hoed the earth.

When the soldiers came to enlist him for the war, he was nowhere to be found. A friend had tipped him off a week before that they might be coming to take him and he had fled his home in preparation. He knew others who had starved or willingly maimed themselves so that they would be able to stay in their village and not conscripted, but that path was not for him.

He hid in the forests, and foraged for food with the skills that the war had taught him against his will. It was no bad thing to be a farmer's son...you knew animals better than most, and the habits that he had observed during his work on the farm served him well in setting traps and snares. His time spent among seeds and plants had taught him where to find the roots and berries that kept him alive.

And every night when he was sure that the dark shapes did not befoul the afternoon sun and when the soldiers had gone to bed, he went back to sit on the hill and dream. He thought it better to sit there, lost in dreams and memories, than be caught up in something that did nothing but steal the hearts and lives of others.

And it was on one cold autumn evening that he saw her.

★★★★★★

For as long as he could remember, he and the other children he knew had been warned about going to the castle. It loomed over the village, an imposing black edifice that was higher than any of the hills that he watched the planes from. He knew the rumors well - there lived a witch there who would skin you alive and eat you. If you even so much as stepped on the road leading there while the moon was out, you would freeze and die.

But the woman that had appeared that night and stood before him was no witch. Nothing could have prepared him for her beauty. Her eyes were a deep shade of red, and the lightest blond hair that you had ever seen crowned in head in white gold. Her skin was pale white, almost alabaster. She wore a black dress that seemed to float off her body, wisp-like, and she moved so lightly it was as if she was floating off the ground.

He froze as she approached. Was this the witch on the castle that he been warned off for as long as he could remember? She certainly didn't look like it. He wasn't sure what to do - run away, or scream in terror, or perhaps even pray for deliverance.

But it turned out that he would need to do none of that. She came up to him, smiled, and spoke. She told him that she had seen him on the hill for as long as she could remember, and that she knew about his love for the sky. She had been watching him all this time, ever since he was a young boy - watched as he had grown and went off to the capital, watched as he had returned to work on the farm and ran away to the woods. She knew him well, and she had an offer for him.

"Come with me." she said, her gaze intent. "I will grant you eternal life, so that you may outlive this foolish war and be able to build what you want desire. I too, wish to fly and that way we will both be able fulfill our dreams someday."

He had never cared much for magic. Science would be what made his dreams come true, give lift to wings of paper and limbs of wood. Not whatever the old wives and superstitious folk in the village spoke of. But seeing her in front of him, crimson eyes boring into his own, he was forced to change his mind somewhat. There was no mortal frame that could contain that impossible beauty...and what she offered certainly went against everything he had studied in school and seen in the air. But eternal life...the power to never die, but beyond that, the way to the sky.

If he had eternity, if he had all the time in the world...then the war didn't matter anymore. He could take as long as he wanted to make his dreams come true. He was tempted despite himself. The long grass on the hill blew slightly in the night wind as he looked at the strange and beautiful woman before him, and he found himself wanting to say yes right there and then and accept her offer. But something else also pulled within him, because he knew that if he acceded to her there would be no turning back.

Sensing the indecision within him, she smiled again, showing her fangs his time, and asked if he would like to come to see the castle. He found himself nodding in agreement.

★★★★★★

She brought him to the castle as the top of the mountain, the same one that he and all the other children of the village had been warned never to go to again and again. And indeed until this day he had never even thought of visiting it once. No matter how high on the mountain it was, it was still on the ground, and what he sought was the sky itself.

It was sparsely appointed, with great halls bereft of everything except the most token of furnishings. There was no one else besides the both of them. Somehow he had imagined a whole bevy of servants at her beck and call, but they walked through the empty corridors their footsteps echoed hollowly.

He followed her silently till they got up on the balcony, where a glimmering crescent moon shone overhead. And that is where she told him how she had watched him look up at the sky, and how she too had followed the planes overhead. She told him of her own dreams and how she had always wanted to fly. He looked at her, pale and angular face lifted to the moon above and lost in fantasy, and saw no witch or immortal vampire but instead a kindred spirit.

Then as she finished she came back to him and asked again. Would he accept eternal life, so that he would be able to make both of their dreams come true? Come live with her in the castle and she would do everything in her power to let him build whatever he wanted to make.

He looked at her and long moments passed. And then he nodded. How could he say no?

She narrowed her eyes and her fangs showed. "Then the pact is sealed."

He raised his throat willingly to her, unafraid. The stories said that it would be endless midnight that awaited him, but something beyond even eternal life called to him. The immortality that poets and warriors alike had sought was to him only a means to an end, nothing more.

Her sharp fangs tore through his throat and he felt her drink long draughts of his life's blood. The last thing he saw before he his eyes flickered and closed was her pale face lit by lunar light and smeared by his blood.

★★★★★★

It was a different life inside the castle. He had never lived by himself in all his short human existence – he was always with his parents, or in a dormitory at school. But now he was left to his devices the entire day – or rather, night. She lived in the rooms above his, and they almost never saw each other.

Of course, he couldn't go out in daylight anymore. But that didn't matter much to him. There was nowhere he wanted to be except here. The dungeons of the castle provided a seemingly endless supply of rats for them to subsist on. They didn't taste like much but he was consumed with a hunger that was beyond blood or the need for survival. He longed for the sky, and he had given up his mortal life (and, if the priests of his village were to be believed any possible hope of redemption) to gain the chance to get there.

Once he had gotten used to his unlife he went back to his house to retrieve the books and the designs that he would need in order to build the planes of his dreams. He allowed himself the luxury of going into his parents' rooms to look at their sleeping faces one final time. What would they think? Their son had not only abandoned their family honor by desertion, but had given up his humanity as well. It didn't really matter to him anymore. It was a new life, a new death, one in which he could devote himself totally and utterly to his dream, without fear of war or age.

Then followed the sleepless nights and days in which he poured over his notes, making wild sketches which slowly turned into more concrete designs. Without the books from the imperial libraries he had to guess at a few things, but he had committed almost every book he had even read on flying to memory and so it was not difficult to compensate for whatever he did not know. And when the theories were done with he was finally ready to begin construction in earnest.

When it came time to build the frame he went up to her chambers to ask her for her help. He needed timber, and wooden struts, and the tools to bind them all together into something more than the sum of their parts. Whatever she asked for, she would smile indulgently and then provide. He didn't know where she got them from and didn't ask – besides, he had a plane to build and a dream to fulfill. With the materials he needed by his side, slowly the machine took shape, strut by strut and beam by beam.

He didn't miss his parents, or his village, or indeed anything of his previous life. He often wondered if there was something wrong with him, if he should feel more sadness, more regret. But then again, why should he? He cared for them, of course, but they have never understood his dreams, never understood why he wanted to take wing and fly into the skies above. They were most likely better off without each other.

★★★★★★

Even immortals need a break now and then, and one day when he felt his eyes smart and his head grow heavy he heard her twinkling laugh call him to him. She insisted they have dinner. It would do him a world of good, she said, and he couldn't find it in himself to refuse. She exerted a strange pull on him – something in her eyes, her face, and her lilting voice – and it was not just because she was his sire in undeath.

So he came to the table and he marveled at eating rats served on fine china with silver cutlery, but that was what she wanted to do, and so they did it. Once was not enough for her, and so every few days she would call him to sup with her. They began to speak after dinner. She told him stories from her long life, wars that were fought, loves that were lost, and he told her about his life in the village, and going to the capital. They avoided all mention of the war or the new kinds of planes that they both so obviously despised. This was a time for rest and sharing before they returned to their respective tasks.

It could have been weeks, or months, or even years that they spent there in that cycle. His nights were filled with work on the plane, and when torpor overtook him he would slump to the ground, insensate. He would get up when his sleep was over and she would call to him and then they would feast together on a rat or two and speak of unlife and flight and everything else.

They grew closer in the time that they spent together. He began to know her moods - the slight shift of her hands before she answered a question, the wrinkling of her nose before she sank her fangs daintily into the furry flesh of her dinner. The toss of her ash blond hair and how her eyes closed in soft pleasure whenever she spoke of flying.

And so one day, greatly daring, he asked her about how she had come to want to fly.

She laughed - that tinkling laugh that he had come to know so well - and asked him why he wanted to know. He didn't exactly know how to reply - did he want to know her better? Understand her more? He was not completely sure himself, so he just said that he was curious.

She tossed her head in her little-girl way and a faraway cast came into her blood-red eyes. Then I'll tell you, she said. Listen well.

It was when she was younger - just a child, really - long before she had become undead, longer still than before he was born. There had been a war - far worse than the war that had brought him to her castle. Her family had been killed, and...oh, how sweet of him to show concern! No, she didn't feel anything anymore. It had been many, many years since, after all.

Where was she? Ah yes, the war. Everyone she had known had died, and somehow she had survived. She had escaped the fires that had laid waste to the city of her birth, and run far, far away - where and how she had no memory of. Finally she had ended up in a mountain somewhere, and had scavenged roots and berries from the earth so as not to die of starvation.

It was a hard and bitter trial for a young girl, and she could remember herself being almost sick from hunger and staggering from tree to tree, desperate to stay alive. And then one day as she looked up at the starry skies above her, she wished that she could fly. The open field of the many lights above seemed to promise freedom from war and pain and hunger and everything else down in the world below.

That was years before she was turned, and even after she had lost her mortality, that memory still lingered within her... the twinkling of the brilliant motes in the starry sky. Most of her kin lose their memories when they become undead, but not her. She didn't say anything about her sire, and he didn't ask. It wasn't important.

It suddenly occurred to him that he had retained all of his own memories. He had awoken the next day in the castle dungeon, much the same person as he had been the night before, just changed irrevocably in one significant way. He asked why and she smiled winsomely at him in reply. If you lost your memories, she replied. how would you make those flying machines?

It was only then that he realized just how old and powerful she must really be. He had never heard of a vampire who could choose what her children in undeath remembered and did not. But he felt no fear from this childlike, innocent and ancient creature before him, just love, affection and loyalty. They were no master and servant, but comrades in search of the same goal. He watched her clean her plate daintily, mopping up the last of the spilled blood with a silk napkin, and felt a sudden burst of caring for her. No matter how long it took, he would make sure they reached the sky.

★★★★★★

He never wondered about the world outside the castle. Perhaps the war had ended, perhaps it had not. It didn't matter to him because even if new planes had appeared, they would be of the new school, all dark metal and frosted glass. He saw how quickly his fellow engineers had been to abandon the planes that he loved, trade the open sky for burning ground. When he had left the capital it was always talk of steel and iron - none of the paper and wood that he would need to break through the clouds and into the reaches of the sky.

He began to talk to her about what he was doing after dinner. How the work on the plane was progressing, how he had managed to put each beam and piece together in new and exciting ways. He described the building of the plane in detail, gesturing with his hands, tracing patterns of connection, construction and creation. She would watch and listen, laughing and clapping her hands in girlish glee. Spurred on by her excitement he would talk on and on, deep into the night, drunk with the passion of relating the story of their dreams coming ever closer to fruition. And she would watch him and smile a secret smile - half that of a parent indulging a child's whimsy, and half that of an accomplice privy to dark secrets. They were both crazed, he knew, intoxicated by an idea that was bigger than either of them.

One day she suggested they take a walk, to the same meadow that he had met her at. He was on a verge of breakthrough - an adjustment to the trinary wing cluster - and he agreed, thinking that the fresh air would do him good.

Everything looked different at night. The long grass swayed in the wind, and the lights of the city shone brightly far away. His parents were probably long dead and buried, as was everyone else he knew. He could barely make out some buildings from where they stood, and he saw some others that he had no knowledge of. The town looked different than he remembered...it was either that it had been rebuilt during or after the war, or that he had simply forgotten how it was supposed to be like. His life there - going to school, talking to the townsfolk, hoeing the fields - seemed like it came from another world.

She watched him silently and when it came time for them to go back, she met him with a question.

"What will you do once you're done?" It was a simple query, but one that she asked with utter conviction. He marveled at her faith in him. Even now as he neared the end of his long nights of toil, he wasn't completely sure if the plane would work in the way that he wanted it to. But she was sure, and that was enough for him.

"I don't know." he replied truthfully. He had never thought had far. They would go to the sky and then that would be the end of it. If he completed the machine, if they survived their maiden flight, then...he guessed that maybe he would build another one, even more beautiful and strong that the last. And then another? What does one do past the limits of a dream? What else is there to do?

That seemed to satisfy her, and with another tinkling laugh she seized his hand and pulled him with her on the past to the castle. He almost stumbled in surprise and she let go of him to twirl amidst the long grass, her skirt billowing and her voice lifted in mirth. He looked at her, amazed, because for all her ancient age she resembled nothing but a village girl at a dance, spinning with carefree grace as the night breeze sent blades of grass up and around them. Then, her impromptu performance finished, she took his hand once more and they both walked back home, a lightness in their step that was not there before.

★★★★★★

The plane was almost complete. One was supposed to have assistants on hand for a launch, but it was only him and her at this point, and so he did everything himself. It seemed strange, even crass, to attempt to ask her to assist - not that she would be able to. She had never evinced even the slightest hint of desire to know how a hang glider functioned or how an airship stayed aloft. He would talk for hours about mechanical functions and wind shear but all she would do was look at him and blink her ageless eyes. She wanted to fly and he was the one who would make it happen, and that was all she needed to know.

It was hard, almost backbreaking work, but the limbs of the undead do not tire or fatigue and so he worked on, night after night. Wood had to be bent into shape, struts fashioned painstakingly out of whatever was on hand, screws and rivets hammered together in the correct manner. He was no carpenter or metalworker and so it took far longer and was much harder than he thought. But it wasn't as it they were in a hurry, after all. They had all the time in the world.

Before he knew it, it was the eve of their maiden flight, and he was beside himself with excitement. The moon was especially full and round that night, and he took at as a good omen. He checked everything again and again but after the fifth time he knew it was time to go. There was a limit to how much preparation one could do, even for something as important as this.

And even with all the checking he had done, he knew something might go wrong. Safety had been his preoccupation – if it didn't work, then they could simply try again. A fall from such a height as they were going to might tax even an immortal's power of regeneration. But there was no way to know until they were actually aloft.

Would it work? He didn't know. He looked on at his handiwork and knew both desperation and pride. A very human sense of worry flashed through him – it had to work, it had to fly...it simply had to! It was easy enough to say that another one could be built, but he had put years (decades?) of sweat and toil into the machine, and the very thought that it would not do what it had been designed to shook him to the core.

A gentle hand tapped his band, and he turned around to look at her expectant face. She took his hands in hers gently but fiercely. He looked down and were they were joined and saw that his were as white too, but stained with machine oil and grease. She flashed him a quick smile and a sharp, knowing glance - co-conspirators, the both of them. Then she pointed to the plane and he nodded. After all these years and struggle - it was finally time.

★★★★★★

He had wanted to go first, but she had insisted they sit in the plane together. And as always she got her way. She had such supreme confidence in his ability that his indecision began to wither and die in the face of her belief. Maybe it would really work. It would go off without a hitch and then they would be both aloft in the sky, their dreams fulfilled. Then the brisk night air blew and he shook his head and brought himself back to reality.

He ran through the checks swiftly - he had made them all a hundred times before - then placed his foot on the accelerator and pushed down. The plane lumbered slowly out of the hangar, its propeller turning. He had barely managed to scrape together a functioning engine from what scrap iron was available, and he had stoked it with just enough coal for them to drop off the sheer face of the castle battlements. From then on it was sink or swim...or rather, fly or fall. He had thought of many other ways to get the plane airborne, but none of them would give him enough lift to remain aloft.

Inch by inch the machine moved, and his heart was in its chest as finally, it teetered on the edge and then fell over it. She cried out in surprise, but he was too busy adjusting dials, and pulling levers to spare even a moment's glance. This was it - either all his calculations worked or in seconds they would smash down on the rocks below. Or maybe they would fly for a while and then smash into the hills - it would be the grandest of ironies if they crashed onto the same place that he had spent so long looking at the sky atop.

They fell towards the earth, faster and faster, and then suddenly the wing flaps tilted and the ailerons aligned and inside of heading downwards they were sailing up. A gust of wind had come just in time and the canvas wings stretched over the wooden frame caught it. And just like that, they were flying.

Flying...flying, finally, finally flying! He couldn't believe it. He gripped the controls tightly and closed his eyes for a brief moment. It was really happening. Looking up at the moon which seemed closer than ever before, and then at the grassy fields which moved swiftly below him, he knew unfathomable joy. It had all been worth it - all the time spent in sketches, in design, in constructing this plane that they were in right now. The wind blew again and he banked left and then right and he shouted out for the sheer pleasure of existence, just because he could.

They spent minutes in the air, spiraling and turning atop the air currents. He shot his passenger a glance and saw her face rapt in ecstasy, unable even to make a sound. He was about to call out to her but stopped at the last moment - he didn't want to interrupt whatever she was feeling. Besides which he had the plane to keep control of.

He was just thinking about heading back to the castle when a judder ran through the plane. His eyes widened in alarm. Something had gone wrong...but what? The undercarriage was secure, and he had made sure that - but it was too late to think about what it was that happened. Their motion through the air slowed and they almost stalled - he shot her a worried glance but he saw no fear in her eyes, only serene curiosity. Even now her faith in him was as strong as ever.

The wind grew stronger and in doing so turned from friend to enemy. From an almost complete stop suddenly they were moving again, but far too fast this time. He struggled to control the plane but the pull of the air proved too strong for him. The wings were the first to go - the same lightness that enabled them to fly in the first place now a liability against the force of the elements. Rips and tears appeared in the fabric, and then the frame itself began to shake and shudder. Slats and struts alike came loose as he watched in horror, the entire plane began to disintegrate around him.

He lost all control of the craft and they veered wildly to the side as it continued to split apart. A final blast of wind proved to be the coup-de-grace and as it ripped through the plane, splintering wood and sending them flying. As they spiraled through the air helplessly he saw her sprout wings - black and leathery, powerful enough to maneuver in mid-air but not strong enough to fly as high as she wanted. Of course - she had been cursed far longer than him, and the tales always spoke of the abilities of vampires to shift their shapes.

He shouted out to her but the wind whipped his words away. He caught a glimpse of her face, mouth pursued in a grim smile, fierce eyes narrowed in determination. What did she -

He knew what she was going to do even before she did it, but he was helpless to stop her. He flailed helplessly in freefall as her body enfolded his and they hurtled earthwards together. They tumbled through the air in what seemed an eternity even longer than their unlife...but when they finally hit the ground her small body shielded his from the worst of the impact.

The shock of the fall had knocked them both apart, and despite her sacrifice he had not escaped unscathed. His vision swam before him and he tottered from side to side, barely retaining consciousness...and even that in time proved a futile battle. He sank down onto the ground, head spinning. But when he finally came to he took one look at her prone form and summoning what strength he had, ran to her. Fighting back tears, he cradled her frail form in his arms and began the long walk back to the castle.

★★★★★★

She lay still, stiller than death - because of course she was already dead. He tried his best to rouse her, alternately shaking her and calling her name, but nothing worked. In the end, afraid to cause more harm than good, he laid her in the bier in her chambers to rest and stole back to his designs and to collect the ruins of the plane that had been supposed to take them to the skies but had merely sent them to the ground.

He spent what seemed like endless nights in blame and self-recrimination. There had to have been a better way...it was the wing design, he knew, too ambitious and spread too wide. But if he didn't have enough lift he couldn't even had held aloft for as long as he had. Maybe he should have gone to town, to the city, sneaked into the library and night and stolen their designs. But he couldn't do that. For even if he had created a machine that did not crash, it would be an ugly thing, black steel and ridged metal, and She would be so sad to have their dreams polluted by war. Far better for her to rest in that state between unlife and true death than to sully their mutual desire in that manner.

The pull of hunger finally broke his reverie, and one day he found himself in a mad dash to the cellar. It was the sitting in a pile of rat corpses - matted fur and stinking blood staining his hands - that brought him back to himself. He looked at himself, disgusted. Enough, he told himself. Even if she never woke, even if it was his fault, he would see their dreams come true.

★★★★★★

He returned to his designs with renewed determination. He began to study birds, bats, insects, anything with wings, anything that could help him achieve his - no, their dreams. He had never fancied himself much of a botanist (he remembered himself being heartily bored by the subject in school) but now each and winged creature seemed to be there to learn from and to teach him something.

Looking at how alive and vibrant the animals around him were, for the first time ever he regretted his decision to embrace eternal life. The beetle's thin wings as they flitted from leaf to leaf, the graceful dance of the butterflies, each delighted him in ways until a few days ago he never would have thought possible. The flitting of bats from place to place was a study in beauty, and the buzz of gnats and wasps music to his ears.

Few birds flew during the night, but he went back to sit on the same hill he knew so well to catch a glimpse of them, silent owl and swift nighthawk both. He closed his eyes in concentration and focus and felt the wind - that same force which could both damn and bless him - caress his face gently, and he knew its swift power and hidden might. And then after that he would go back to the castle to draw and sketch and design some more. In his mind lines and curves began to take shape, intersecting and transforming into another vision, faster and stronger than what he had built before.

And whenever his drive faltered and his resolve wavered he would go to her chambers and look upon her wan face smiling gently in repose. Grief and regret would assault him once more, and he would swear again to reach the skies no matter how long it took. If not for him, then for her...for the both of them.

★★★★★★

He took even more care this time. The spiders had taught him the secret of their webs, and the hummingbirds their ways of motion. He had redesigned the entire frame from scratch, knocking out the top and replacing it with another. The only things that he had kept were the canvas wings, for even all his studies had not shown him a better way to catch the breeze and remain aloft.

He was of two minds this time as he wheeled the plane atop the battlements once more. He was more confident now, but at the same time. If he died as well...then they would both have lost their lives to no end. But once again there was no way to tell it unless he tried.

Again the sudden plummet earthwards, but this time he had no need to depend upon stray gusts of wind for propulsion. He had learnt enough from the insects and animals he had studied so intently, and so this time the frame flexed and bent and glided it flew through the sky

It worked! It worked! His happiness at his success was marred only by the knowledge that she was not there to join him. But it was a step forwards. He had reached their goal, and now all that remained was for her to awake and share in it. But what if she never woke? If she remained in that place between sleep and death forever? He pushed aside any thought of that and steered the plane home.

★★★★★★

He built another, and then another, and then another after that. Each flew better and more easily before. He would take each out to test them and each time he was a bird among the air currents, flying and leaping with the same grace as the avians whose wing shapes he had copied. He flew through the evening sky and close to the moon in all its phases - waxing, waning, gibbous - over the town of his birth which looked so different from above, over grassy fields and even farther away, so far he could even see the lights of the capital. He had conquered the air, made it is servant, and was subject to its fickle whims no longer.

But despite all his successes she would never wake. Each night he would kneel by her, hoping, even praying, but she still remained silent and unmoving. Finally in desperation he took to telling her about the planes as he had before. Everything that he now knew, from the mysteries of the living things that he had learnt from to how the his new hasp designs and engines combined to create new and better ways to take wing. But still she lay there in stillness with a silent smile upon her face.

One day he ran out of supplies and could do no more. She had never told him where she managed to procure everything that he needed for his designs - the lightweight wood that bent as he needed it to, the canvas pieces and rivets of brass and copper - it had all suddenly just appeared whenever he wanted. Just like with everything about her, he never asked and she never told him. He supposed that he could go out into the woods, steal an axe from the town and fell trees to make another machine...but what would be the point? She was still asleep and would not wake no matter what he did. He had mastered the sky but even that dream was for naught without her to share it.

He fell back into that same reverie that he had gone through before when he had but this time it was not hunger that broke its hold on him. One night he simply found himself back in the hangar, staring at his latest creation. The sky...so distant for so long, but now well within his grasp. Except that in many ways it was even further than ever before.

★★★★★★

For lack of anything better to do, he found himself walking the meadows late at night.

Maybe it was better if they had never met. If she was still half-alive, wandering through the fields late at night. He would be long dead and gone by now. If he had never been turned, what would he have done? Gone back to the academy, most likely. Perhaps he would have been drafted into the war, and then he would have lost his life at the end of a stray bullet or cannon shell. Or he would have survived and married and had children, grown old and died.

Then he would never have made those flying machines, and she never would have fallen, and he would be resting in the cool damp earth instead of standing where he had first met her.

He plucked a stray blade of grass from the ground. Maybe he should leave the castle, and seek out another one of her kind - he or she might know what to do. She had never told him of other vampires, and he didn't know the first thing about beginning a search. And even if he met one, what would he say? Would they even want to speak to him, or offer their assistance? For so long all of his being had been consumed by flight - dreams and the longing and love of it. He knew nothing else and had never wanted to. But all that knowledge and passion would not bring her back from wherever she was now.

He walked closer to the town and saw it spread out before him. It had been many, many years since but from the castle it somehow looked the same as always. No one had ever come up to visit, and he supposed that they told the same legends that they always had - of the flesh-eating witch and the werewolves that lurked in the forest. Eternal life meant that

★★★★★★

He went back to sit by her side, his devotion the only thing he could offer at this point. The nights passed, and he was deep in another vigil when it happened.

He had his eyes closed when suddenly he felt the touch of a hand upon his face. His eyes flew open in amazement. It couldn't be - but it was. She was sitting up and regarding him steadily, as beautiful as he remembered.

"You've done it." she said simply. It wasn't a question, it was a statement. She could see the answer in his eyes, so he simply nodded. What else was there to say? It was like that on that night hundreds of years ago, when she had asked and he had answered. He had accomplished their mutual goal many years before. All that he had waited for was for her to awaken to share in it.

"Take me there." He would only be too glad to. He took her hand in hers and together they walked to the hangar.

★★★★★★

She took her place in the seat with the same propriety that she had on that night years ago which he couldn't even really

116

remember. But now confidence replaced indecision, and he could feel the same way about himself as she felt about him. He grinned at her and she smiled back so widely that her fangs showed. The time had finally come.

What had been so difficult now was so easy, and he took the now-familiar sudden plummet down from the castle walls at such a clip that she shrieked in amazement. Her surprise was music to his ears as he sent the plane into, and then a quick turn sideways to boost their velocity somewhat, and then he pulled at the levers and the wings aligned and they went up and up and up –

– until they were soaring far above the castle that was their home, and the clouds were brushing their faces. The night breeze blew cold around them, and

They flew, and she laughed, and it was laughter like he had never heard from her before. The sweet tinkle of her voice climbed high into elation, and he heard it match

They knew the sweet taste of their dreams coming true.

The moon shone brighter than it ever had, and it was so close...so close it seemed just inches away. Mindful of the limits of even his finest creation, he banked down once they had reached their zenith, but and out of the corner of his eye he saw her outstretched hand try to touch it.

He looked back at her and their eyes met. He saw hers shining in the moonlight, and her lips parted in half a laugh and smile. They were flying, and they were more alive than they ever had been or ever would be.

Nightbird Calling

THE BOY WAS waiting for her at the window.

He was waiting for many reasons. Because he was bored, for one - he was afflicted with the insatiable curiosity for life that is the illness of all boys his age, and the pursuits of home could only amuse his young soul so much. Because it was an excuse to come up to the window, to look down on the City below, the High Market and the Pillars...he did have an excellent view of from his windowsill, and he loved to sit and watch the world go by - as much sitting and watching a boy could do. And because he wanted to get away from the homework that he was supposed to do.

But mainly he was waiting because he knew she would come.

A boy's life has all sorts of things in it - games, assorted pranks and mischief, scoldings, the odious and dreaded school. Friends, enemies (easily made and destroyed, lost and found) Secrets that were dear one day and useless the next.

But it so happened that in a life so tumultuous - as all boys' lives will be - this particular boy wanted a little bit of routine. He wanted to be sure of something, to know that come what may, a certain thing would happen at a certain time. It gave him a sense of security, of comfort. He wanted, most of all, to have something he could count on. And so he went up to the window to wait.

It was a long time before she arrived, but he didn't mind. He had waited longer before, it's just that he didn't really remember doing so, and if he did he wouldn't really have minded either. So he sat on the windowsill, watching the birds fly past and the leaves tumble down, listening to the sound of the wind in trees, waiting.

And after a while, he began to hear the sound of silent wings. He wasn't sure how one could hear silence, but he did. It you were to ask him, he might tell you that it was a kind of whispery sound, a bit like rats in the attic, if the attic was your mind and the rats were the kind of voice that kept on telling you to eat the vegetables that you didn't want to. But then again he might not.

She landed on the branch right next to the window, preened slightly and looked straight at him. He smiled back.

"Evening...early aren't you?" Her voice was always different, always strange. It never sounded the same way twice.

The boy shook his head. "No, I'm not. The sun hasn't gone down yet."

She paused to shake her head, stretching her arms out ever so slightly to shake away the dust from her journey. "Why, so it hasn't. We have plenty of time, I think." There was a brief silence in which both she and the boy were bathed in stillness.

He waited expectantly for her. "So what shall we do today?"

Turning back from gazing at the setting sun, she favored him with a rare smile. "We could go down to the Pillars. I have something to do there."

"Alright then, let's go." The boy didn't really like going there in particular...actually, while he was with her, he didn't like or mind going anywhere in particular. It was enough that they were going somewhere, and she was going with him.

"Come. We don't want to be late, and it's a long flight." She beckoned to him, and since it was only a short distance to the branch and her outstretched hand, he jumped from the windowsill, confident that he wouldn't fall. He did slip a little on the surface of the wood, but she was there to steady him, and soon they were ready.

"Hold on. I'll be flying a little low today." He nodded to show that he knew, and they were off.

★★★★★★

The spires were always a sight to see, from his window or up close. They stood so high and proud and black, silhouetted by the morning sun, that he was in awe of them no matter how many times he passed by them, whether it was on foot as he walked to school or in the air as he was now.

He clung to her back tightly as she swooped and dived between each tall tower. His short hair was whipped back by the wind and he shrieked in delight as they swung past and over the City.

They flew over more of the busy streets and scattered buildings and he peered over her shoulders excitedly. He saw people spread out below him like so many ants and watched in fascination as they began their day. He was so high above all of them, and they were so far below.

No matter how many times they did this, he never grew tired of it. He greeted each trip with the same childish enthusiasm - eyes open in wonder as he took each sight and sound and smell. Such is the innocence of children.

He bent over her shoulder to ask her where she was going, but after a second pulled back. He didn't need to ask, he knew. They were going to where they always went.

★★★★★★

They passed by the High Market with all its hustle and bustle, the fountains in the Main Square as they bubbled and frothed, and soared on beyond the hills and the rivers that were outside the city. The works of man slowly gave way to the greens and blues of nature. Cobblestones and brick roads turning to forests and rivers. And finally they were there.

With a great backwatering of wings she came to a stop, the blast of air from her landing sending fallen leaves and pebbles flying. He slid off her feathery back carefully. Brushing a few stray feathers from his clothes, he looked around. He had been here many times already, but he never grew tired of visiting.

It was a graveyard on the outskirts of the City. Headstones dotted the grassy knoll where they found themselves, and there was a mausoleum further on inside which he had never been in.

Others avoided the place, thinking it full of ill omens, bad luck or both, but he loved it. It was quiet, and peaceful, and not one else ever came here, so he could be alone with her for as long as he wanted to be.

The dawn light painted the grey stones a pale yellow-white and the leaves and the grass glimmered with a faint radiance. They had come here at many times of the day, from bright afternoon to shadowy dusk, but it was the early morning that he always liked the best.

He left her alone for a while as he wandered through the gravestones, trying and failing to read each inscription. He touched one after the other, marveling at their smooth texture of the marble and their raised inscriptions. She didn't like to be disturbed during her first few minutes here, and he didn't ask why.

He liked how she never asked him anything, and how he didn't need to ask anything either. With the adults and the other children there were always questions, questions and more questions.

What did you do at school today? Where are you going later? What would you like to eat? He didn't see why they couldn't understand that some things were just the way they were because they were, and that no amount of talking or questioning would make it otherwise.

She understood, though, and he liked that about her as well. She just sat, and flew, and did whatever it is that she was meant to do, without talking about it or questioning anything. That was just how she was.

He looked back and she saw that she was almost ready. She had this way of raising her head and looking about that told him that. He ran back to her, small feet scattering stray leaves left and right, and he was happy to see her smile in return. It was time to do what they had come here to do.

He followed her as she went to each grave in turn. She raised her wings, her eyes would change, and then the words on the stones would flare bright red. He didn't know exactly what it was that she was doing, only that he enjoyed watching her and that it was somehow necessary.

And once again unlike the adults he knew she never minded if he stopped halfway to play with some fallen leaves or to sit beneath the shade of a nearby tree. There would be no nagging about how he was lazy, or he should help, or being chased back into the house to do his never-ending pile of homework. He could watch as she worked, and that was exactly what he did - until a stray squirrel attracted his attention and he chased after it.

The squirrel didn't hold his attention for more than a few minutes, and then after that it was a fallen branch which he swung against a nearby tree with a satisfying crack, and then after that a stone that he kicked down into a stream, delighting in the sound of its splash into water.

But then he grew suddenly tired as children are wont to do, and he slumped down in the shade of a tree. He half-dozed, half-slept beneath the swaying branches, and he let his tired mind and body slip off into the world of dreams and memories.

★★★★★★

He remembered when he first met her.

It was a school day, but not a very good one. First of all, it had rained, and he had forgotten to bring his old shoes, instead choosing to wear his new leather ones. They had gotten all dirty from trudging through the mud and he knew that his mother would yell at him.

Then he somehow forgot his homework when he was sure that he had packed it the night before. The teacher had made him stand in the corner and the whole class had laughed at him while his cheeks blushed red. It was unfair...so unfair! He knew that he had put his books into the bag. He just knew it.

Finally, an older boy had bumped into him and took the money that he had been saving to buy a new book. He had shouted in indignation and rushed into the other youth, trying vainly to get it back, but all he had gotten was a punch in the stomach for his troubles.

The day dragged on and when school finally ended he trudged home miserably, his new shoes sinking into the brown muck that caked the streets. His mother did indeed shout at him for the state his shoes were in, and he just stood there sadly for a good ten minutes. It was a repeat of the afternoon with his homework - being scolded for something that wasn't even really his fault.

Worn out and tired and all he wanted to do was to sleep, but even his warm and comfy bed could not console him. He tossed and turned for a while and then, finding no solace in slumber, he moved to sit at the windowsill instead.

And then he saw her. One moment it was a clear and sunny day and the next a dark shape had blotted out the sun. She swooped down with a sudden motion and looked at him, not unkindly.

"What's wrong, little boy?" she asked.

If he was older he might have been afraid of her. But youth lends one a certain invincibility, and he couldn't believe this majestic creature meant him any harm. If he was older still, then he might have run shrieking to get his mother, or to the nearest temple to call a priest. But he was just a young boy and as such knew nothing of the injunctions against speaking to one such as her.

Her great black wings seemed natural because no one had ever told him they were not. Her eyes were as fierce as an eagle's but at the same time as gentle as a dove's. Her voice was unlike anything he had heard before...but then he had not heard many things in his young life. She was fierce and terrible, beautiful and silent all at once.

So instead of running away or calling for his mother, he smiled at her and reached a hand out in greeting. His small fingers curled around her claws and he found their scaly surface somehow reassuring.

He told her all about his horrible day - about the shoes, the rain, the older boy, the teacher - everything. She listened intently, nodding at key points, and never interrupted even a single time.

When he was done the boy heaved a sigh of relief. He felt so much better. He was not yet old enough to understand the easing of the soul that having someone listen without judgment can bring. He just knew that he felt good. Then, remembering his manners, he thanked her.

She smiled in return, and closed her talons gently around his hand. Then with a great sweep of her wings she was gone once more.

★★★★★★

She came back every day after that.

Sometimes he would talk and she would listen - about his day at school, about the things they did, about the other boys and girls. And sometimes they would just spend time together, looking out onto the City below. They couldn't see much from his windowsill, but they could see enough, and he would point out each landmark excitedly and she would nod and smile at every cry and gasp he made.

After a while she began to take him with her. He was scared at first - she flew so high and so fast! - but he gradually got used to it. She was gentle with the first few flights until he found her sudden takeoffs and landings to be as natural to him as walking. They circled his house first, until he was comfortable, and then the spires, then the High Market, and then they flew to the outskirts of the City and beyond.

Every day he began to look forwards to when she would come. The time (late afternoon, usually) when he would be back from school, and how he would hurry through his homework so he could be ready when she appeared near his windowsill. When the clock struck for the fifth time in the town square his ears would prick up, because that meant only a few more turns of the sundial before it was time for them to leave.

He never asked his parents about her, or told them what they were doing. They were always busy in any case - his father at the smithy and his mother baking, cooking and generally keeping the house in order. They assumed that he was somewhere playing with the other boys or amusing himself with something else and he didn't see why he should tell them otherwise.

After weeks of flying with her the visits became the highlight of his day. There was nothing else in his life that would compare - not his schoolwork, not the running through the open fields outside the temple, not even the sweet cakes that his parents would sometimes buy back home from the stores in town. School was a boring routine that he had to endure, and all his chores were just things to get through until he could spend time with her. He looked forwards to when she would arrive and her black wings would block out the sun and then they would take off to parts unknown.

She brought him all over the City and to many other places besides. They would soar high above spires and mountains with equal ease, riding the air currents like birds. They went to the rivers and he would watch in awe at how she would deftly spear fish after fish with her claws, then eat them in a few fast, savage bites.

They visited meadows filled with strange fruit and she had cautioned him never to pluck, and the ruins of buildings that he had never known or read about. Upon her back he saw parts of the world that had forever remained unknown to him.

But she always returned to the graveyard. She had brought him here on one of their early visits and he had loved it, asking her to bring him back again. She had smiled, nodded and complied, and though they visited many other lands, it was always there that they both would return to.

He was too young to know about duty, or purpose. He only knew that she always went there, and where she went, he followed.

She would tend to the graves in her own way, and he would play in the tall grass and in between the shade of the trees and watch her, and he was as content as only a young boy with no cares could be.

★★★★★★

For a time, it seemed like those days would go on forever. But things change.

It was a day like another other. He had gotten up in the morning and eaten his breakfast of crusty bread, then taken his bag and gone to school. The teachers droned on and the boys played rowdily at lunchtime and after the school day was done he made his way back home.

But today something was different. People looked at him as he walked back through the cobbled roads, and then they would turn their heads away, whispering. There was sighing and pointing and much shaking of heads. He was confused. What was going on?

It was when he neared his house that he truly sensed something was wrong. There was a crowd of people near it, talking amongst themselves, though they parted when he approached. They looked at him concernedly but he paid them no mind - he wanted to know what had happened, and he was sure his parents could tell him.

But when he got into the house he saw his father sitting at the table - he never sat at the table unless he was eating dinner - with his head in his hands. The priest was there, and as he entered the holy man cast a compassionate glance his way.

"What's wrong? Where is mot..."

And for the first time the boy realized that his mother was nowhere in sight.

With the voice of one who has had to deliver bad news many times before, the holy man laid a gentle hand on the youth's shoulder.

"Your mother...your mother isn't with us anymore."

The priest's lined face and voice seemed a thousand miles away as he spoke. A cart had fallen somewhere above the High Road, filled with stones fresh from the quarry.

An accident, he said. It wasn't anyone's fault. No one could have foreseen the ropes fraying and snapping when it took a sharp turn. And no one could have known that it was just that moment when his mother had exited the bakery and walked onto the street.

The stones had fallen from the cart and crushed her in seconds.

No, no...it couldn't be true. He dashed into the kitchen, expecting to see his mother bustling around the oven, her shrill voice chastising him for something or other. He would endure a hundred scoldings and thousand dirty shoes, if only she would be there.

But the kitchen was empty. The spice bottles were on their racks and the rolling pin was set against the wall in the same position that she always left it. A fine coating of flour covered everything, the only evidence that she had even been there in the morning in the first place.

The boy looked around wildly, frantically, and the priest walked slowly towards him, intending to soothe his troubled spirits. But suddenly his father moved forwards towards his son and spoke sternly to him.

"That's enough of that, now. Quiet down and don't trouble the priest anymore." He reached forwards to steady his son's trembling shoulders, heedless of the effect that his words had on the young boy.

His father was a simple man, and he didn't realize that that was possibly the worst thing he could have done to console his frantic son. Quiet down...quiet down! That was the last thing in the world that he wanted to do. He wanted to scream, to shout his defiance at a cruel world that would take away his loved one from him.

So that is what he did. The boy let out a cry that shook the rafters and dashed out of the house, screaming. His father's calloused hands tried to restrain him but even the long hours at the forge were no match for the strength borne of grief and desperation.

He barreled through the crowd outside his house and ran down the streets not knowing or caring where he was going. All he could feel was the ache in his mind and his body, a dull pain that sunk deep into him. He couldn't think or feel properly...it seemed like the entire world had come askew.

But somewhere through the haze in his mind a thought came to him - find her. She would know what to do, she would fix it. She could listen, and then and look at him in that way of hers, and then things would be ok. She would know where his mother was.

But where could she be? It was the late afternoon and so he could go to the windowsill, but there was everyone else blocking his way. His father would stop him for sure and take him back his room and lock the door and then he would never be able to find her.

The graveyard. That was it. She was always there, and after those many many flights above the City he knew the way. He started running to where he knew she would be.

★★★★★★

It was a long way to the graveyard on foot, longer than he had ever thought possible. But even if he had known it was could never be done he would still have run on, past the spires and the High Market and the rivers and trees. His feet grew torn and blistered and his breath ragged with fatigue, but still he ran on, driven by something more than himself, a need that could never be met by words or platitudes.

She was there, as he knew she would be, looking at each gravestone with wings outstretched. She glanced at him as he approached, shoulders heaving with exhaustion, and he knew by her eyes that she understood what had happened, as he knew she would.

She came over to him and stretched out a taloned wing, and that gesture suddenly unlocked the gates that the priest's hand had been unable to.

He sank to his feet, sobbing. Where there had been screams before now there were only tears. Grief and loss surged through him, and her wings made a feathered canopy as he cried and cried and cried.

And then finally the racking sobs wound down into teary-eyed sniffles he raised his head and asked her the question that humanity itself had wondered for forever.

"Why do people have to die? Why can't you bring them back?"

As a child he didn't understand - couldn't understand - the impossibility of what he asked for. He only knew that his mother was gone and wouldn't come back and that there was only person in the whole world who could do anything about it. He couldn't have known that what he asked for was beyond blasphemy, beyond countenance, that to even do so would send the priest of the temple into a blind panic. He simply asked out of pain and the need to end it.

She reared up above him, and he backed away, terrified - for here She was revealed in all Her terrible glory. The wings had spread back, dark shapes against the night sky, the talons raked the ground and the tail lashed like a beast uncaged. Then She spoke, and it was flame and sorrow, regret and stillness at all once.

"There is nothing in this world that can forestall death. Even I do not have this power. I bring the souls to the gate, nothing more."

For an endless moment the worlds parted and for a moment he saw what she must see each time her wings spread in front of the graves - light and darkness swirling in unfathomable patterns, sounds that echoed through one's being with such force that simply listening to them changed you. The world beyond yawned before him, and both abyss and radiance shone back from it.

Then it was gone, and he looked at up her, tears still streaking his face. His young mind could not understand the words that he heard, or the images he had seen, but his soul told him otherwise. He knew the truth of what she said, and it hurt it even more than the loss of his mother had.

She reached down with one taloned hand and flicked each tear from his cheek. The points of her claws scraped ever so gently over his naked skin, and then her great wings caught him as his eyes closed and he fell into them.

★★★★★★

She never came back after that day. When he came to had been deposited in front of his house, and she was nowhere to be found. He had dried his tears and gone inside and slept for a night and a day.

The funeral was a simple affair. His father had learned his lesson (from the priest, perhaps) and chose not to remonstrate with his son any longer. Instead he left him well alone and let the boy mourn their mutual loss in his own way. The funeral procession wound down the streets that he knew so well from the air, and they seemed so long - much longer than when he flew above the City, the wind in his hair, his hands on her feathered back.

With the reality of pain and loss in front of him those days seemed so far away and long ago. Someone had to keep house and cook the meals and make sure everything ran properly, and with his father still at work that duty fell to him. What with everything that was going on, he never even realized that she was gone until a few weeks had passed.

At first he was upset, and then indignant and then after that, furious. Where did she go? How could she just simply leave him here like that? What about all the time they had spent together? But as time passed the flames of his rage cooled and hardened like the steel on his father's forge and grew into a feeling that when he was older he would know was called resignation.

Though he never forgot her, other things began to take their place. As his grief waned he began to go out and play with the other boys - what his parents thought he was doing in all the time he spent with her. He took walks in the grassy fields outside the City, and went to the High Market to buy fruits and meat. He circled the spires that he had once passed in the air on foot, marveling at how high they really were.

And when he came of age and went to the temple to learn the prayers that each young man was expected to know, he came to understand what an honor it was that one of the Elder Ones had come to his windowsill and flew with him on her shoulders. Who had even shown him a glimpse of the other world, the twilight realm that even the highest of the high priests had not seen in more than twenty years of devout service.

His father, after the prescribed two years of mourning, took another wife, someone unlike his previous one. She was short where his mother had been tall, silent where she had been loud. The boy - now halfway to manhood - didn't hate her, nor did he love her. She was just there, another member of the house. The cakes she baked weren't as good as the ones that his mother made, but he didn't expect them to be. Her voice was never raised in anger, but then again, neither did her hands pick him up when he fell, or brush the dust of his clothes and ruffle his hair. She was someone else entirely, and he could accept that.

The years passed and the boy grew into a youth, and then into a man. He began to wonder anew if she would come to see him. They still lived in the same house, and sometimes when the evening approached he would glance at the windowsill where he used to wait for her every day, hoping to hear the sound of great wings. But that never came, and little by little his hopes died.

It soon came to the question of his chosen vocation. He thought of being a smith like his father, but somehow the thought of beating heated metal into hard shapes day after day held little appeal to him. He could perhaps become a carpenter, or shoemaker. Maybe even a scribe · in recent years he had gotten better at his lessons and his teachers had begun suggesting that that might be a good choice for him. If joined the temple he might see her again· ut then again, he might not. And even if he did, she might not want to see him. Too many questions to answer, with no way to answer them.

He took to walking around the town square, unsure and uncertain. He would look at the sky and past the spires and remember the days when they would dive and spin past their tall, tall arches and – and then he would shake his head violently and try to be rid of the memories that seemed to only pull him back and away from the practical considerations of what he had to do to survive. It was too long ago, and those times had little or nothing to do with who and what he was now.

And so he thought, but suddenly one day as he was meandering aimlessly as usual through the city streets a flash of memory thundered through him, and he remembered the glimpse that he had of the other world, and what it had meant. The lightless night that lay beyond death. The vision of the lands beyond that one day everyone would go to.

Something seized him, and he began to visit the sick, and ill and the dying. He knelt by them and heard their stories, he bathed their heads in water and held their cold and clammy hands. And when the mendicants had left their beds and the priests had said their prayers, it was his words that stopped their shaking, his fingers on their faces which soothed grimaces of pain into calm and peaceful smiles.

He became someone who did not fear death, and because he did not, people came from towns around to hear him speak and to look on at this man who visited morgue and sickbed with equal impunity. When they looked into his eyes they saw no judgment or censure, but only compassion, wisdom and resolve.

He spoke to them of death, of dying and what lay after. And his voice rang with such conviction that they believed him, he who had not passed through the ranks of any temple nor wore the robes of any priest, but who as a young child had ridden on the shoulders of Death's handmaiden herself.

He himself never worried or wasted a moment in regret or recrimination, though there were sorrows and joys aplenty in his long life. He never took a wife nor had children, but spent each day in service to those who needed him. But from the day that he first spoke to the ill and the dying, he asked the same questions no longer.

Because he knew that one day, when he himself was at death's door, she would come. And her wings would spread wide and eyes grow darker than night, her talons would close over his frail and fragile hands, and together they would fly once more over the City and its black spires, the High Market and the people below, past rivers and forests and fields...fly to that dawn lit graveyard and beyond.

Ends and Beginnings

I HAVE COME home. But it is nothing like I remember.

Everything is the same and yet it is not. The castle looms in the distance, a grey shadow nested among valleys and mountains. It comes closer and stays still with every footstep I take. Things should be as I have left them, but they are not, and I am a traveler once more, walking through rivers and plains that I have seen but never really noticed until now.

I move forwards not really on foot but through time and space as well. The forests part and the mountains grow taller and then recede into the distance.

It is all as I left it, but nothing is quite the same. In all my journeys I have never been back before, but now as I approach my home in the distance from a different time and direction I begin to muse on the futility of it all. It doesn't quite matter what I do here.

Perhaps it is just as well. After all it is all already over. There is just one last thing to be done before I say farewell for good.

★★★★★★

The castle is exactly as it is in my memory, each painting, pillar and statue where it used to be. The shadows cast by the draperies are the same as when I last saw them, but yet they cannot be, because it has been far too long. More inconsistencies. Everything that should be, is, and yet it is not.

It is all too excruciatingly familiar. I walk past as fast as I am able, not wanting to tarry a moment longer. It is not that they are too painful to see, but there is a certain wrongness about them that I am anxious to be rid of.

But something about the wall hangings and embroidered palings calls to me, and against my will I find myself walking through the corridors of old. My pace slows and I am transported once again to ballroom dances, to tea parties and chandelier-lit evenings. Before the wars, before my travels, and before what has come to pass.

I cannot deny that it tugs at me, at things long ago left buried and forgotten. I want to forget and yet I cannot. Maybe that is why she has done what she has.

There is no way to know. And at that thought my legs once again pick up speed and bring me forwards. Before I know it I am passing the carpets of the antechambers, the stairs of my first duel, the climb to the minarets and beyond, where I know she is waiting. It does not take me long to get to where I am going, and before long the doors of the great hall loom in front of me. I open them.

She is sitting there, sipping tea, smiling quietly to herself, unchanged as the day I first saw her. I am relieved and disappointed at the same time.

I bow. "My lady." Because after all this time I am still her knight, sworn to serve. That is why I am here. To bring her back to her senses, when she has clearly taken leave of them. Or has she? I know what she has done, but not its full extent. Maybe there is yet time to change her mind.

She doesn't turn to me, or acknowledge me in any way at all. Is she angry? Tired? Uncaring? I don't know and it does not matter. Seconds turn to minutes and we stand there, standing, sitting, staring. Waiting.

"Why have you come?" She is the one to break the silence. In past times she was always the one who spoke first, and that at least hasn't changed.

"You know why." And it is true. We both know why. I have come to render one last service, to make her see the truth of her actions.

"My lady, your castle is empty. The courtiers have all gone. The grounds have not been swept. Everywhere the storm rages, but it is just that you do not see it." All this and more I know to be true. And it is more than likely she knows as well. But nevertheless some things have to be said.

"But everything is the way it is meant to be. Nothing is gone, and nothing has broken. Don't you see?" She smiles and gestures around her. And in many ways it is as she has said. Everything IS the same. But at the same time it is not.

I stare helplessly at her. How can I make her see? The end of the world has come, but by her will, at least in this place alone, it is eternally forestalled. And she is possessed of nothing if not a strong will. When the hordes came so many years ago, it was her strength of the mind that raised the shield wall. When the floods threatened the land it was her power once again that broke them. In this place at least, nothing changes without her permission.

Even as everything else decays and is destroyed, she will endure unchanging, should she wish so. Which is the crux of the matter. If she wishes so, and she does.

As I look on, watching, waiting, praying, hoping, staring at her hopelessly, it suddenly dawns upon me. I cannot do anything. If she does not wish it to end, it will not end.

"Do you remember?" Her voice breaks my reverie.

She smiles and I smile back, and suddenly we are no longer there, but among the meadows of the past, the unlit skies and the marshes we traveled to when the realm was whole. And once when things were too busy and hectic, the tea party just for the two of us that she tore a hole in two dimensions for, just so no one would know we were there. I know that she is in the same place I am, that our thoughts are travelling the same pathways to the places that we knew in a past life. All that is there slips away, and all that was past comes back.

Lifetimes pass in that instant – for we have both lived many of them – and then we are back, in that eternity that still awaits destruction.

She stands. "I wish to go to the uppermost tower. You will come with me." It's an order, not a request. I stand to attend her, and it is like old times once more, master and servant. We both walk out slowly, her skirts trailing on the floor and my feet keeping pace with her.

The way to the tower is long, but we pass it in silence. What else needs to be said?

I know why she has come here, because I have often come here for the same reasons myself. For solitude and solace, away from the seemingly endless cares and troubles of a realm that was never settled, even in times of peace. Always a dispute to be resolved, always an affair to be mediated and looked over. But here...here we could be alone, and have some time to ourselves. Time to rest and recover and recollect before the next crisis loomed.

Up here you can see everything. Far and near, the lands spread out before us. Forest, woodlands, rivers, mountains – as far as the eye could see and beyond. Our world, that we protected for a thousand thousand years, until the day came that everything was over.

What brought the end? None of really knew. There were storms that had always raged at the borders of the world, but the prophets always told us that they would never break the barriers that our ancestors had erected at the cost of their lives. And for a long, long time they didn't. There were powerful ones, but none that could break the shield wall that my lady had strengthened with her will. None like the world breaking typhoon that had shattered all pretense of safety and that now threatened to consume...HAD consumed everything.

And so today as we stand on the battlements all we can see is nothing. The world beyond the barriers was gone, an empty yawning chasm of oblivion. All that remained was this small bubble that stood within the chaos and destruction, the remains of a kingdom that once stretched beyond vast plains and towering mountains. All gone but for her unyielding will.

She stands tall and silent on the parapet in the waning light, and I am struck again by how beautiful she is. This is not the first time I have looked upon her and thought this. There was the northern campaign, where the dawn shaded her in whites and yellows which set off her the satin of dress, and the time in the desert where the swirling sands brought out the color of her eyes. I am seized by a sudden desire to go over to her and hold her by her slim shoulders, but I restrain myself. Such actions are not befitting of one sworn to protect.

"Do you miss it?" she says suddenly, gesturing. "All this. The realm."

"No." I am surprised by my own answer. But it is true. Everything must die someday, and I am no exception. Perhaps she can defy time and fate eternally, but at what cost? Living alone in a castle with only one occupant, constantly surrounded by mementos and remembrances of the past and better times. It seems no paradise to me but rather a purgatory of her own devising.

But in the end I am only her servant. I have known her for countless years, but I cannot read her thoughts or her emotions, only make guesses that often prove wrong - for she as capricious as she is wise. When the snows came to the northlands instead of melting them she transmuted the ice floes into a million snowflakes ("the better to entertain the children with" she said) When the volcanoes erupted in a shower of rocks and lava she sent the knights to bring in every last flaming stone to make sculptures with. In her service to her and our lost realm my blade has felled thousands of foes, but I have often wondered at what she keeps hidden within. All that power and will, forever a mystery to me.

What is going through her mind as she looks out on all of before, on a world that has already ended? I stand and I watch, and I wait. That is all I can do. She knows my thoughts on the matter, and we understand each other too well for me to say them again.

Eternity passes.

I can feel it even before it happens. A silent shaking in my bones and in all of reality. I turn to face her, unbelieving, and she smiles at me.

"It is done." I don't know what to say. A thousand questions form and die between us as our eyes meet. But once again nothing needs to be said. She has let go.

I walk forwards and take her hand. Before us the realm crumbles as all that was kept at bay rushes forwards. The black wisps of the storm spin and whirl through everything, and though I cannot see them I know that the seas are churning, forests swaying and breaking apart. The mountains split and are torn asunder and the vast plains which we once rode through catch fire and burn. Everything is coming to an end.

What has happened to make her decide I shall never know. It does not matter. She bows her head and closes her eyes and I can see no tears. There do not need to be any, for the end of the world does not need to be a sad thing.

Prism Reflections

HE WAS BORED.

It was a sunny day and there were plenty of things to do. He could go to the park. That was always fun. Or he could take the bus down to town and browse through the shops - not buy anything, just look. But he didn't really want to do either of those things.

He was waiting for her to come over and she was late. As usual.

He didn't know why he put up with her. Really he didn't. It's not that there weren't lots of other girls in the class that he could have asked out instead. Any one of them would have - ah, who was he kidding? No one else would have even given him the time of day. He sighed and rolled over, getting grass stains all over his white shirt.

It was probably because she was the only other girl in class who shared his interest in all the old things. Transceivers that didn't work, batteries with no juice, all sorts of gadgets that no one knew anything about. One day he had noticed her looking at a broken transmitter and asked her where she got it. She told him that it was from the junkyard nearby and on impulse he had asked if she'd like to go with him to look at it. She smiled and said she would.

That was the first of many trips, and the first time she was late. He had waited for half an hour near his house, growing alternately frustrated, anxious, irritated and was verging on anger when she nearly ran into him, a bundle of barely suppressed energy. After they had disentangled themselves they had made their way to the nearest junkyard and spent nearly half the day picking through the rubble, picking

He got up and kicked a nearby rock into a nearby stream, then checked the settings on his hover bike, then finally just lay on the grass and looked up into the sky. Late. Again.

An impish face framed by bangs suddenly popped into his vision. Upside-down, it smiled that smile that he had come to know so well.

He was more than a bit startled but didn't let it show. Instead, he kept his face neutral. "You're late." he said.

"Yes I am." she replied, as if daring him to say something else. He didn't take the bait. She jumped back and twirled a bit while he gave the controls on his bike another once over.

"Well then, shall we go?" he moved over to start the bike only to see her looking at him curiously.

"Go where?"

"The junkyard, of course. We were supposed to go there yesterday."

Now it was her turn to kick a stray rock into the stream. She turned on one foot and spun around again. "I don't wanna."

He suppressed a sigh. Yesterday she was practically champing at the bit to go, asking him every 15 minutes, and today she didn't want to? "Well, I'm going if you aren't."

She pouted at him and with a single deft motion leapt onto the back seat of the bike. "Ok, let's go then."

He shook his head. He could never deal with her quick changes of mood and had decided not to even try. "Alright then." He gunned the engine and they were off.

★★★★★★

He decided to take the scenic route this time. It was only the late morning and they would have plenty of time to spend there later. Besides, he was on his bike now - it wasn't as it they had to walk there.

They passed the promontory out by the rocks and he turned his head to look at the massive hunks of metal that lay there. The teachers at school told him that here was where one of the fiercest battles before the war was fought, and countless robots had been destroyed in it. What they saw today was only a fraction of the war machines that had once battled each other and torn both earth and shore apart.

The surf had come in over the years, pooling in and around the rusted arms of the behemoths of old, and the passage of time had rusted and eroded what had once been gleaming metal. Fishes swam in and out of them, and algae had begun to grow on the dented surfaces.

He always felt strange whenever he passed them. As a child he had played among the fingers and hands of the iron giants without a care in the world, jumping down from high atop the broken shoulders of the robots until his father shouted at him to stop because it was too dangerous. It was only later in school that he learnt of their history. How they had blown cities apart and slaughtered thousands - no, millions, their armaments raining fire and destruction down on almost every human on the planet. How they had almost destroyed the world.

She didn't appear to care about any of that, though. She chattered excitedly to him about everything under the sun - what they were going to do later, what they had learned in class yesterday, what her friends thought of this or that - a near-constant stream of speech that never seemed to run out or run dry.

And when she ran out of steam (which he thought could never ever happen) she heaved a contented sigh and laid her head gently on his back. He gulped slightly in shock and pleasure and rode on. A stiff breeze sprang up, and as he made a sharp turn around a bend in the road the exhaust from the bike kicked up a spray of sea water. It washed over them in a fine mist, stray droplets dotting his face as he closed his eyes against them.

The road wound past trees, bushes and beyond the ocean graveyard of the iron giants. He made a last turning into the forest that would lead to the junkyard and cast a last glance at the metal hulks which dotted the shoreline. Maybe it was just his imagination but he thought they knew where he was going and were saying goodbye...or hello.

★★★★★★

It had taken them the better part of an hour to get to the junkyard, and when they got there she jumped off the bike and rushed towards it as if she couldn't wait to get started. Which she probably couldn't.

She was the only girl he ever knew that was actually interested in any of this stuff. He knew why he was, of course - it was his father's research. Growing up with someone who talked of nothing but lens refraction indexes and concave and convex arrays all day, you grew them like it a bit despite yourself. He knew other kids who didn't, though. There was Barron next door whose mother was a botanist and he swore that he would never have anything to do with plants. He and the other boys in class would always be away catching fish or chasing girls or whatever it was that they wanted to do.

Why was she interested, then? He wouldn't admit it to himself but he never dared ask, for fear of scaring her away. That he would come off as too pushy or too inquisitive and then she would pout or yell and never come with him to the junkyard again. So he didn't ask, but he often wondered why.

They spent the better part of the day looking through the junk for things - specifically, reflectors. Prism reflectors. His father had told him that back in the days of the war, the giant war machines that now littered the landscape used those lenses to focus their energy beams. There were a huge variety of them, in colors ranging from cerulean to emerald - a kaleidoscope of hues and tints scattered among the rest of the scrap like so many glittering jewels.

She loved them, that much he could tell. She would dance atop the rubble and pick them out one by one, her excited gaze darting from one shiny object to another. He, on the other hand, tried to be more scientific about it. Remembering what his father had told him, he compared one to another slowly, taking his time to point out the differences in size, shape and even texture. After a few minutes she shot him an annoyed glance and he stopped talking, suitably chastised. To her it was more of a game than a study, more about pleasure than science.

As the day died down and they grew tired they cleared a space free of rubble and sat down together. He wasn't just tired - he was really exhausted. Not that he would admit it. Glancing out of the corner of his eye, he wondered how she could keep it up.

"Don't you think they're beautiful?" she asked, holding one up to the late afternoon sun. The sunlight shone through it, refracting into myriad rays that scattered and sparkled all around them.

He wasn't sure he could agree. The lens were well-made, of course, and they reflected the light well enough. But he couldn't help but remember their deadly nature, how they were made to kill and not be used as jewelry or trinkets. Or even harmless entertainment on a lazy summer afternoon.

But still...sitting here with her, legs dangling from a stray tank cannon, he could almost pretend that harsh reality of the past wasn't real and didn't really exist. Everything they had learnt in school seemed distant and faraway, and the reality was him sitting with her with the sun shining down and looking at that pretty white dress she wore.

Her voice brought him back to the present. "You didn't answer my question." she pouted at him.

"Well...I guess they are? In a way?" he was being indecisive and he knew it. He laughed half-heartedly, putting a hand on the back of his head, and she reached over to give him a push.

"You're avoiding the question! Answer! Properly this time!"

"They are." And they were. They may have been used to kill in the past, but this time they were just...lenses. Lenses that made a beautiful display when the light passed through them.

The day wore down, and they continued in much the same way as they had before - scavenging around the junk to find old things, beautiful things. After a while he was content to just sit quietly as she flitted from place to place, picking up lens after lens and sorting them into piles. She had gotten her second wind, it seemed. She didn't seem to grow tired and when evening made its inevitable approach he took her back on the bike before it got too late.

She didn't lean against his back this time but instead fastened her hands securely around his waist instead. He wasn't sure which he preferred, but he sure wasn't complaining.

★★★★★★

They went back to the junkyard quite a few times after that. They tried a few other places - the scrapheap near to the sea, and another smaller one farther inland. They were fun to explore for a while - although he almost got lost once in some caves that she wanted to try going into, which ended in a shouting match that neither won or lost. But in the end they always went back to the same place.

They didn't search for the same things each time either. Sometimes it was other gadgets, other relics of the war. He took a particular interest in magnetic discs for a while, seeing them spin and hover inches above the ground. He even once threw them in the water to see how far they could go and smiled as he saw them skip across the pond. Three was his record, seven if he turned them on before throwing. She liked the little spark plugs that they sometimes found as they dug through the scrap - they lit up and burnt with a fierce flame for a while before going dark again. Neither of them really knew what they were for, but it was fun to collect them and play with them and then set them down again when the fun was over.

But she always went back to the reflectors and lens - picking them up, tossing them around, looking at them this way and that. He warned her that if she threw them too high they might break, but she just laughed and told him that he worried too much about nothing. And it seemed that she was right. No matter how badly she treated them - and he once caught her pitching them down some rocks by the side of the collected junk - it seemed that however she handled them, they would never break.

Then one day while he was searching through some boxes he felt a tap on his shoulder. He turned to see her winking at him, a reflector lens held in her open palm.

"Here you go, a present for you. For putting up with me."

He was going to say that it was no chore putting up with her but he thought the better of it. No sense in giving her ideas.

"Why this one?" he asked.

"It's special, you dummy! Can't you see?" she pointed at it.

He looked, then looked again. He didn't see what was so special about it. It looked like all the other reflectors - a bright orange hexagon, chipped here and there in a few places.

her expectant face blinked at him and he found himself saying "Thanks."

She frowned "You avoided the question again. You didn't tell me why it was special."

Because you gave it to me? Because it's the first one on the heap? So many possible answers to that question, and he struggled frantically to find one that wouldn't result in him being smacked on the head. He was still thinking mightily when her knuckles connected with his nose.

It wasn't a punch - somewhere between a push and a shove - but it sent him onto his haunches anyway. He backed away from her glaring face. He blinked in terror and stammered out a reply.

"Okay, okay, it's special! It's special but I can't see why!"

She laughed and tossed the reflector at him. He caught it reflexively and held it up to the waning sunlight. She was right... it WAS special. The rays of the sun hit it bit differently than they did any of the others. It glinted just a little less and shone just a little more than all the others.

He put it in his pocket and thanked her, and she sketched a little bow and went back to searching for more lenses. Evening was fast approaching and so they finished up when they could. He hadn't taken the hover bike this time, so they took the short way home.

There were no fallen giant robots to see on the way back, only trees and bushes, so she contented himself with watching her as she danced down the mossy path and laughed at nothing in particular.

★★★★★★

It was another slow and lazy day, and since he just felt like it he took the hover bike over to the broken bridge down by the river and spent the whole day there. Just because he could.

She hadn't been coming to school the last few days, but that was normal for her. She sometimes took a week or so off, and no one knew where she had gone or why. Maybe she was sick...could she even get sick? He guessed that even she could.

He rolled over to get a better look at the sky and felt something in his pocket. The reflector. He fished it out and held it up, squinting at it.

She was right. Everything did look prettier through the lens. Even chipped and broken like this one was, the sunlight hit it and fanned out into several images of black hair and five eyes looking down at him and –

It was her again. This time he couldn't help but be more than a little startled, especially as she had appeared so suddenly.

She pointed at him, laughing. "I got you there! You looked so stupid!"

He pushed the reflector back into his pocket and scowled. Alright, so he had gotten a little surprised. Who could blame him?

"Do you want to go to the junkyard today?"

"No, that's ok. Let's just hang out here for a while." He blinked. Not go to the junkyard? She must be sicker than he thought. But he thought it prudent not to mention that.

She dangled her feet in the nearby stream. There were more fishes here than at the ruins that they passed by, and she pulled her feet back and giggled as one particularly large one brushed by them. Sunlight shone down on the water and it glimmered with a light that was not unlike one of those reflectors - except that these lights pooled and flowed and rushed on in a flow that soon drifted out of sight.

He caught himself staring at her while she skipped and played among the rocks and fishes. She was wearing another dress today - a pastel-hued one that had gotten wet at the hem from the water. Not as nice as the white one from before but pretty all the same.

"What's wrong with you?" she asked, looking at him curiously.

"Nothing." He couldn't just TELL her that he enjoyed watching her frolic. Even if it was the truth.

"Nothing? You're staring at me!" And that was true, even though he had tried his best not to let her notice.

She stuck out his tongue at him and he almost stuck his out in return...except he didn't. Why? Some part of him thought that if he did, she would win, and he didn't want that to happen. She got enough of a rise of him most times that he didn't feel like giving this once.

So what he did do? He made a flying leap for her and she shrieked in startled joy, and they spent the next few minutes chasing each other around the river. He almost had her at certain points but just when he thought his hands would close around her shoulders she would spin and laugh and he would be clutching at air.

It went on until she slipped on a stray stone and fell backwards – and he was there to catch her. He blushed in sudden embarrassment, acutely aware of how close she was, but the next second she had slipped out of his grasp, giggling, like one of the fishes in the stream.

That was somehow the signal to stop and they put out their clothes on the grass, waiting for the sun to come and dry them. The afternoon wore on and they sat and whiled away the time talking, and before they knew it was almost evening.

★★★★★★

Nighttime fell and they were at the junkyard again. They didn't normally come so late but somehow today they had felt like it. There was really not much point in coming when the sun wasn't out – there wasn't enough light to find anything at all – but somehow they were here.

She ran to the top of the heap as always and he trailed behind her. They sorted through some piles just for the fun of it and poked through a few other things but both of them knew that they were wasting their time. So when she pulled him up to their favorite spot at the cannon, he let himself be manhandled into a sitting position as she plunked herself down besides him.

It had grown darker and he could barely make out his hand in front of him, but she knew she was sitting not inches away and that fact comforted him a great deal. He heard rather than saw her scoot back a bit.

"Do you ever think about what things were like before the war?" she asked suddenly, turning to him.

The moonlight shone in her eyes, more brilliant than any reflector he had found or would ever find. He swallowed. What should he do? Should he lean forwards? Backwards? Neither?

This was worse than the time at the river...at least he knew what to do then. Now he was utterly and totally confused.

Before he could decide she had pulled herself away again and directed her attention at the stars in the sky. He didn't know whether he was disappointed or relieved, but he cast his glance skyward as well.

So many stars. It was as if the night sky itself was a giant reflector and each star a pinprick of light on its vast black canvas. They sat and stared for what seemed like an eternity before she turned towards him with that curious look that he had come to know so well.

"How many do you think there are?" she asked.

What kind of a question was that? They were stars! You couldn't count them? He had heard his father remark on more than one occasion that there could be millions

But that was the kind of girl she was - asking questions that you couldn't very well answer. He looked at her and there was something in her eyes this time that told him she was completely serious and wouldn't take "no" or "maybe" for an answer.

"I don't know." he replied truthfully. Seeing her face twist in a frown, he hastily added "but I think there are just too many to count. Maybe there's no end to them."

She seemed to like that answer a lot more. Absently she took his hand and for some reason he wasn't embarrassed this time. They sat in silence for a while, admiring the night sky, and gazed at the stars as time seemed to go on forever.

★★★★★★

That was the last time they met for many years.

It was only a month later he heard the news. He had assumed that she was sick again, or had gone off somewhere. She used to do that after that one week - just disappear from school and everywhere else. He always assumed that she would come back when she was ready - it was her, after all. But it was only when the teacher told the class that he knew she had moved.

He was torn apart but he never admitted it to anyone. Nor to himself. He went to school as normal and talked with his father and even visited the scrap heaps to find more reflectors from time to time, but everything was different without her there, and after a while he stopped doing even that. There was no fun in collecting things without her around. He amused himself with some new devices that he had found - electric coils and gearwheels - but it just wasn't the same.

Time passed and when graduation rolled around the hats came off he shouted with the best of them, but who he really wanted to shout at was her. Why did you leave? Where did you go? What am I going to do without you? But she wasn't there and so all he had to content himself was the celebratory punch (tame, but still good) and the praise and cheers of everyone else around him. Both did little to lift his mood.

There were other girls, but none like her. None that he could share prims reflectors with, and late nights spent looking at the night sky. None who would pop out of nowhere with a smile or a frown or a wink. There was a nurse, kind and gentle, and a scientist, brilliant and passionate, but none like her. None even remotely like her.

At university he threw himself into his work and did incredibly well, far outstripping even his talented father, who looked on with admiration and more than a little surprise. At the awards ceremony the older man clapped the hardest but his eyes seemed to be asking his son on stage where all this drive to succeed came from. He was hard pressed to answer himself. And when they had gotten the communication relays up and running and one could make and receive calls anywhere that had a system set up, he had forgotten all about her. Or so he thought.

He kept the reflector that she had given him, the one that had fallen and chipped itself on that day by the riverside, so long ago and faraway. When he was bored he would take it out and press on it, flipping it through his fingers and holding it up to the sun. Once he even threw it as high as he could, but caught it before it hit the ground. He didn't have her luck with these things and if it broke for real...he didn't even want to think about it.

He never lost it, even though he lost his keycard (to the eternal consternation of his housekeeper), and his hover bike controls and everything else. Somehow it always managed to find its way back into his pockets, or a kind stranger would pick it up and give it back to him with a "is this yours?" He would mumble his thanks and push the lens back into his pocket with a sigh of relief.

In the summer after graduation he joined a research team working on lens, and within a couple of years he was leading it. He didn't know it was his natural aptitude or inhuman drive or just because he loved lenses because they reminded him of her. Probably all of the above.

After years of research his team finally found out how the reflectors actually worked. They focused light from a pulsed energy array into a single focal point, amplifying the output of the primary streams many times over. The implications were astounding. As long as the correct lens was used, it was theoretically possible to multiply any energy source as long as it was powered by lasers or something similar.

The news sent waves through the research community. Energy! They never seemed to have enough of it, that most precious and valuable of resources. The dams could be built now, and the new towns, and one day maybe even the orbital arrays...it all was possible now. All they had to do now was design better energy emission technology, and of course, find more lenses.

More lenses. That was the problem. There never seemed to be enough to go around, and those that they did manage to find weren't good enough. They had to be refined, and refining was costly (more energy!) and that was another problem – they needed to use energy to perhaps create more energy, with no guarantee that they would get back more than they spent. But it was his job to do something about that. So he researched more deeply than ever, determined to unravel the secrets of the small glass discs that could do so much.

Once in the midst of a presentation an image of her sprang into his mind, holding a lens up to the sun, and he had to block it out before he was consumed with memory. After it was over he went over to some stairs at the back that no one used and cried.

He never forgot about her, and sometimes when he was alone he allowed himself to wonder whether she ever forgot about him. He was filled with both pain and loneliness, tinged with no small amount of frustration. Where was she? Where could she have gone? Why hadn't she tried to contact him – conveniently forgetting that he should have perhaps tried to contact her as well. He knew her name, but he had no idea where she had gone to, and while she was in class she had never told anyone. Maybe they were all excuses or maybe they were real reasons, but either way he was here and she was...nobody knew where.

★★★★★★

More time passed and he left the town he was brought up in to move to the city. It was an obvious choice – all the most cutting-edge research was conducted there, and they had the equipment and devices that he needed. Other scientists also wanted him near where they were excavating the last of the ruins, so the assessments could be made quickly without having to transport the parts back to HQ. Why would he say no?

Moving was a hustle and bustle of activity, but he left it all to his assistants. There were new theorems that needed polished, methods that needed refining, and he was too busy to bother with mundane affairs like where to stay and what to eat. Leave that to the others and he would do what he was best at.

They had begun to contract their work out to scavenger teams. There were just too many lenses which needed processing, and though they had diggers and boring machines now, the sheer amount of them necessitated some outside support. Besides, there was a limit to what automation could do. They still needed a human eye to discern which were worth bringing back and which could be just ground down to make prism dust to power the machines. Some were junk, but some were so high quality that a single lens could power over six lasers. But put the wrong one and the lasers would backfire and the whole thing would go kaput. They couldn't risk mistaking one for the other.

There had been talk about the workbenches and water coolers of a single scavenger who could somehow outdo all the other teams, who was so good that he or she could find a hundred good lenses in the time it took for everyone else to find ten. He paid it no mind. It was just more idle conversation. He had always been a loner in school and the years hadn't changed that in the least. Let them talk about whatever they wanted to. He had other, better things to do, more research to complete, more equations to solve.

His assistants really wanted him to meet this person though. They begged and pleaded and told him all about how it would help the image of the institute, it would show the common folk how they were involved and not just white shirts. Why not, they asked. It would only take a few minutes of his time. He resisted as best as he could but after two whole weeks of badgering he finally gave in. It would save him the time if he just talked to this person rather than putting up with his assistants, he reasoned. Best use of resources and all that.

It was her, of course.

Her hair was longer now, but she wore it in a new style, a single ponytail down her back. She was taller, but she still had the same impish smile and look in her eyes. He stood stock-still, dumbfounded.

"Hi! Remember me?" Of course he had. He hadn't forgotten for a single day. He couldn't.

There were so many things he wanted to say, so many things he wanted to ask. Where had she gone? What was she doing now - ok no, that was obvious, she was a lens scavenger now -but why was she doing that? Where had she been all these years, and -

But before he could do any of them she had whipped out a bag from behind her back with the same quick motions that he knew so well. He moved forwards to look, eager despite himself. Could it be -

And it was. Prims reflectors. So many of them, sparkling like a gemstone hoard. All perfectly shaped and of the highest quality.

"How did you find these?" he managed to stammer out.

"I looked." That was her all over again. She never answered with two words when one would suffice.

"How many of them are there?"

She smiled and winked. "As many as there are stars in the sky."

The things they could do with them! The machines they could make. The lasers they could refine, the things they could build...the orbital arrays seemed closer than ever.

But as he looked up from the bag at her all those things vanished from his mind. He opened his mouth to speak but she just pressed the bag into his hands and left, the spring in her step conjuring images of days gone by.

He didn't follow, because he knew he would be seeing her again. She'd go find more lenses, more reflectors, and he would make new and better machines, and then she'd find reflectors for those as well. He should have known that she would never really leave him. All these years spent experimenting with one prism array after the other, sorting, finding, checking...how many of those lenses were those that she had found and that had found their way to him? She had always been there on the other side of the world, sending them his way.

He looked back at the contents of the bag and he saw myriad possibilities. Machines that could move earth and soil, bend rivers from their course and seed the clouds with rain.He saw her fingers picking, sorting, catching and tossing the shiny shards of glass and knew that they had been among countless junkyards and thousands of scrapheaps, searching, finding and searching once more.

He saw the past, and the future, her bright eyes and nimble hands. He saw the science that he had studied and how he could improve the lives of so many more people, how it could help bring back a world that had once been torn and ravaged by war. He saw her again.

And all of them sparkled more brightly than the stars in the sky.

Gears and Flowers

THE BOY ALWAYS knew how long it would take to get there. It was 10 minutes by hover bike, and then another 5 or so if he walked fast. If there was no underbrush in the way, and he went by where the grass was thick and long, he would be there in no time.

She was watering the garden as usual. Her long blonde hair was pulled back by the breeze into a yellow flag that streamed into the sky.

He had brought flowers, freshly plucked from the riverbank. He didn't know if she would like them but they were so many of them on his way past the river, reds, greens and blues in a shimmering display, that it seemed like a shame not to pick them, so he did.

He started running when he saw her. He couldn't help himself. She was so beautiful, standing there, still, calm, almost devoid of motion except the movement of the can. She seemed as much part of the garden as the flowers, or the bugs, or the sunshine.

But somehow when he got there, all his youthful enthusiasm left him, leaving only shyness behind. He managed a "Hi."

She smiled. "Hello." She was a girl...woman? Something somewhere in between - of few words.

She didn't say anything after that and there was no need to. He did all the talking, running around, scampering here and there, rolling the mud because unlike the other grown-ups (was she a grown-up? he didn't know) she never told him not to. He told her stories, some true, some made-up. About how he and his friends had dug up a secret treasure the other day, and buried it somewhere else the next. About how Roy fell off his Dad's hover bike and everyone laughed at him. He was going to school next year and he was sure it was going to be great.

What he liked best is that she listened, and smiled, and didn't scold or lecture or tell him to do (or not do) anything. She just smiled and watered the garden.

Hours passed, and the sky turned from blue to green to gold and finally to the time he liked best, a mix of orange and black and grey. He would have to leave soon which he hated but it was ok because there was always tomorrow.

When it was time to go home he waved "bye!" and shot off like a rocket, all his shyness forgotten. He would be back the next day, and the day after that, until the summer was over. And then maybe the next summer. And the one after that. But like all boys he lived in the moment and had no thought for the morrow, and his eyes darted from one wonder to another - the trees! the sky! the clouds! - on his way through the roads back the girl was soon forgotten.

★★★★★★

The boy knew the path well, even though it had changed a bit. The grass no longer grew thick and long, but rather short and fine, since the rains had changed their patterns. He had a new bike and so it was a few minutes less as well.

But he still ran along the path to her house, not even stopping for flowers this time, because his legs were longer and his body was bigger and he had energy to spare. He ran in a steady stream of movement, feet pounding on the earth, one-two, one-two, for the sheer joy of being alive and going to see her.

She was there, looking not a day older. She still watered the garden with the same slight motions as before, still straightened and smiled at him when he came by. The wind was not as strong as before but when it did pick up it would toss her hair much like he remembered, and he would lose his train of thought in mid-sentence, caught up in each strand as it was flew hither and thither.

He had always wondered what he did with the flowers and one day he had plucked up his courage and asked her. The blooms that she grew were different from all those that were in town, with colors and smells which delighted the senses. She answered that they were sold at the markets in other places, and he simply nodded. He didn't think to ask what she did with the money, and she didn't tell him.

He ran back the same way he had come. He would be back the next day, and the day after next. Life was simple, and things were good.

★★★★★★

As he grew older the valley around him seemed to come into more and more life. Perhaps it was that he had never noticed before because he was too caught up with her and the stories he would tell, the blue sky above and the wind in her hair. But now he could see that the flowers grew not only by the bank but by the hillside as well, and the trees were a different color each time he came by. He was growing and as he grew not just him, but everything else grew bigger as well.

School grew longer, and his visits grew shorter. He no longer ran up the path by the river, instead walking slowly by, lost in thought. There was more now than just visits and flowers and her. His lessons had broadened his view of the world, and he now knew of more things than just his town and the others around them.

A long time ago fire and war had split and ravaged the land, and people had died and whole countries destroyed. Everything that they had now had been born after that terrible devastation. The valley and the stream and the trees...it hadn't been here before. None of it had been. It had grown only many, many years after all that death and terror.

He didn't know what to make of that. The children around him at school laughed and played and ran as always, and he did all those things with them, but in his heart something had changed. The boy now knew what death was, even if he hadn't seen it himself. He knew that once upon the time the world was not always bright and free and clear. And that knowledge changed him.

But she never changed. She saw him, she smiled, and she listened to whatever he might be saying at the moment. She continued to water the garden as she always had. Different blooms, this time, to suit the season, but the green-blue eyes, the same movements as she turned from one flower to another - those stayed the same. He didn't tell her about what he had learned at school, and as always, she didn't ask.

He walked back the same way as he had come before, and this time he forgot to look at the flowers and the trees and the sky. Somehow he felt better - he always felt better whenever he saw her - but still there remained some unease. He didn't quite know what to make of it, and so he just continued to walk back.

★★★★★★

The youth walked up the bank slowly and carelessly. He was in no hurry to get there. His hover bike was a new model and this time it brought him so close to the woods that he didn't even need to walk that much.

By now he knew enough to realize that she wasn't like any other girl he knew. Her hair never seemed to grow longer, nor did it seem to need to be cut. She wasn't like his mother or his sister or any of the girls at his school. She treated him the same, year after year, whereas other people seemed to treat him differently day by day. (He wondered if this was what the adults called "growing up.")

She was different. Different from anyone he knew. And yet she was always the same, always smiling, always listening, never far from the garden. He didn't know what it was that made her different and for some reason he found that he didn't care.

The stories he told now were different as well. He began to speak about the future. About what he would do when school was over and in the days to come. There were boats down by the river that needed fixing. After all, hover bikes didn't work on water! Old Man Jacob was always talking about how they should go something about the houses that had been abandoned near the coast...and then maybe the next year they could go to the City, and then –

And then, and then, and then. What had always been a place of the present only suddenly had a future, filled with things to come. There was more than the house and the valley, now. There was a world that had not yet come into being, that only existed in dreams and words. But she listened all the same, as she always had.

And smiled. But she would also begin to ask questions as well. How do you fix the boats? How far is the city? When are you getting a new bike?

They spoke (or rather most of the time he did) for what seemed like hours, and when the time came for him to go back he would drag his feet and find just one more question to ask and one more reply to hear. But he knew that eventually he would have to go home and no matter how he tried to put that reality off the sky would darken and as night fell he knew that he would have to leave.

It was on one of the autumn evenings, running back across the stream, that he realized that he loved her. That he always had, ever since he was a boy. And with that realization all the trees and flowers and surroundings began to take on a new light. He looked up and the sky was pitch black, with stars dotted, and he couldn't ever recall when he had felt so happy.

★★★★★★

He ran up the stream as he had always done, but not for a long time. This time he carried flowers, picked from the hill instead of by the stream. He realized that it would take him longer to get there without the hover bike but it didn't matter, he would just run. He didn't want to spoil the flowers, and if he took the bike they would have been carried away by its exhaust.

He didn't know how to ask what he was going to ask. He had turned over the idea and the question in his head a hundred times, no, a thousand. It seemed like the best idea in the world, and then seconds later, the worst. But he had to do it.

The paths he had walked so often now seemed so long and unfamiliar, the pebbles and stones that were strewn here and there by the elements all strangers to him. He made his way slowly to the house.

She was there as always, watering the flowers. He took a deep breath, plucked up his courage and spoke the words.

"If you would...if you would go with me to the dance?"

She smiled and shook her head.

He was torn. He was sure she would say yes. He knew she would say no. He didn't know what he thought, or thought he thought. He just knew that he had to ask and that he couldn't have been prepared for whatever she might have said.

Turning so that she could not see his tears, he started off home. He thought that maybe he could have said it different, or said it better. But maybe he couldn't have, and she would have said no regardless. He thought that...no, he couldn't think of anything. Except maybe how disappointed he was.

She stared after him, still smiling, flowers in her hands. He couldn't bear to turn around, and so he didn't.

★★★★★★

The man had not been back for many years. There was no need to. So he didn't know why he was walking back the same path he had walked and run down so many times before.

It took only five minutes to get here now. The new hover bikes had boosters that were strong enough to get past whatever foliage happened to be in the way. He thought of taking the scenic route but decided against it at the last minute. He just didn't have the time to spare anymore.

He had grown up since the last time he was here. He knew enough to know that she wasn't human - could not be. Down in the city - or rather, Iverness (there were many cities, and more were being rebuilt everyday) they taught that some of what they found were relics from the war. Maybe she was one of them. She could be an android, or a humanoid robot, or anything in between. They couldn't be sure yet what she was, but they were working on it.

Somehow, it didn't matter one bit. He was back to apologize. Some time ago he had walked away when he shouldn't have, and it was time to make amends for that.

He came up to the house at a brisk pace. The flowers were different this year - he hadn't stopped to see them for some time, and when he did he was amazed by the difference in their colors. She was there, waiting as usual.

He looked her straight in the eye. "I'm sorry." It said everything that he wanted.

She smiled back. "It's ok."

Time passed for a while, and looking at her in the evening sunlight, he wondered about her smile. Why was she always smiling? How could she? When they found out – if they ever found out – what she was, would they ever figure out her smile? Somehow he didn't think so.

The time for stories and questions and answers was past, so he simply closed his eyes and took his leave. The way back was shorter than he remembered, or maybe his legs were longer.

★★★★★★

It had been some time again, but not as long as the last. He stopped the bike where he had stopped it when he was a boy, and walked the rest of the way for old times' sake.

The valley was beautiful in the fall. This time he made sure to notice the color and shade of every bloom and leaf and tree as the dappled light of autumn bathed it. He would not be back for some time, and he wanted to commit everything to memory in case he forgot. Not that he ever would. He ignored the voice that said that he might never come back. He would – he would. He just didn't know when.

The road leading to the house had changed in the years since the last time he had been here. For one, it was longer than he remembered. It seemed to wind on forever, crossing past rivers and streams that he knew he should know but he didn't. Memory was and is a fickle thing, and the man/boy was learning that.

He came up the house and she was there as always. There were less bushes now, and less flowers, but she was standing there with the watering can as always. There was no wind, this time, and so her hair did not flutter in the breeze. He came up to her slowly.

"I'm getting married. I'd like you to be at my wedding." It was easier to say that he thought. He had rehearsed it a few times, unlike his last disastrous confession, and that had helped.

"I can't leave the garden." He knew that she would say that, and it hurt, but she was smiling as she said it, and that made it easier.

164

"I won't come back for some time." She nodded as if she already knew.

They spent some time staring at each other. He suddenly felt like telling her everything, just like he had as a boy - about his wife-to-be, about the house they were planning to buy, the move they were going to make. But he didn't say anything. He just stood there, staring, as the fall leaves swirled around them.

She smiled at him as he turned to leave. On the way back he passed flowers that he didn't know, and trees that were much, much taller than he remembered. His eyes darted to and fro like they had many years ago as he tried to lose himself in each and every detail. So caught up was he in the activity that he didn't even notice when he had arrived at the bike. He mounted it in a swift motion and headed home.

★★★★★★

"Daddy, Daddy, you're too slow!" This time there were two sets of footprints along the wooded trails, one large and one small.

Nothing had changed. In this place it seemed that time had stopped forever and would never continue on. He had grown older, and wiser, and sadder, but the valley seemed locked in time. He made his way slowly along the road, his son skipping ahead of time.

Halfway to the house he stopped to look around and realized that no - all around him things were different. Drones had begun to flitter around the trees, pruning and watering them. The changed weather patterns were easy enough to spot with his trained eyes. And the flower blooms were even richer this time around. Technology had worked its magic and changed even this sanctuary.

He wasn't sure if he was happy or not at the way things were, and so he tread the same paths again in no small amount of doubt and confusion. Before long he was at the house.

She was there as usual, not watering the plants this time, but standing and waiting for them. How she knew they would be coming he had no idea. He stared at her as his young son laughed and pranced around her, much as he had done himself so many years before. He gamboled and shrieked and ran here and there and the flowers had never looked more beautiful.

She stood, looking straight at him, smiling. He felt at that moment that the world could end again and she would still be smiling. Her hair blew in the wind like always, and he was taken back many, many years to a time long ago but not so far away.

He didn't know what to say. Perhaps he didn't even need to say anything. He opened his mouth to speak but at that moment his son came barreling at his legs and he was pushed down onto to ground, the wind knocked out of him.

She laughed. He had never heard her laugh before.

Smiling sheepishly, he got up, brushing grass from his legs. He stood up, took his son's hand, and said goodbye. She nodded slightly.

The way home was just as long as he remembered. He took some time to look at the trees with his son, pointing out the names of every flower and leaf and delighting in his exuberant cries as the younger male touched and poked at each one. The sky spread out above them, a clear and distant blue, and as he stooped to boost the young boy onto his back he could not recall ever feeling happier.

★★★★★★

The paths had all been washed away by the floods of the previous year. There was no safe place for him to walk, but it didn't matter. The exhaust of the bike glowed a cool green light as it sailed easily above the rocky ground.

His hover bike made a gentle landing - he didn't even have to move a finger. He had finished the alterations only a year ago, and now he could operate it almost completely remotely.

Its control was fine enough to make it right to the deepest part of the valley, skirting all the fallen foliage that the rains had dislodged.

The house was gone. So was the garden. It had been too many years since, and people had begun to move away from the area long before the nature had finished the job that man had started. The old man walked slowly to where he knew she was. He had to - at his age and in his condition he could only move a step at a time, and so he hobbled to where she waited.

She stood there the same way she always stood. He raised a trembling head to look at her and started to speak.

"I just want to you know that...that..." he couldn't finish the sentence.

She walked towards him and took his hand. Her blonde hair flowed into the breeze like he remembered, and her green-blue eyes were the same hue that he had seen when he was a child. He didn't actually need to say anything, he knew. She would understand as she always did.

At his age he knew all about her. Or thought he did. After 20 years they had finally gotten the satellite links up and running, and the orbital archives could be accessed. He had read manuals, watched holodisks, talked to all the experts. None of them explained her. Nothing explained her smile.

He didn't know why he had made the long trip back here, other than the fact that he had to see her one last time before he died. Even with the new implants that he had received the previous year, he wouldn't last long at his age. He knew that, and that was why he had come back.

He stared at her and she looked back, smiling, and he felt once again that he had millions of things to tell her. All about how they had finally terraformed most of the areas that had been devastated by the war. How his wife had taken sick and died, and his son and daughter had moved to the cities to become scientists like him. How they had found so many androids but none that looked like her - if she was even one.

And this time it was the simple fragility of the body that rendered him unable to speak. He opened his mouth to continue but all that came out was a cough, and then another, and then another. He began to collapse but she moved towards and gently held his frame as it was racked by shudders and when they had run its course he looked up to see her there. Smiling.

★★★★★★

BEGINNING TECHNICAL READOUT AND ANALYSIS.

SUBJECT: A-1, OLDER MALE.

SUBJECT REQUIRES ATTENTION. CHECKING PRIMARY OBJECTIVES...

PRIMARY OBJECTIVE: PLANTS HAVE BEEN WATERED. FLOWERS COLLECTED. FULFILLED

SECONDARY OBJECTIVE: RESPOND TO SUBJECT'S QUERIES TO BEST OF ABILITY. FULFILLED.

TRINARY OBJECTIVE: LISTEN TO SUBJECT TO BEST OF ABILITY. FULFILLED.

UNIT HAS FULFILLED ALL OBJECTIVES. AWAITING FURTHER INSTRUCTIONS.

★★★★★★

Ship of Light

TODAY IS THE first day I start work aboard the Melchessoir. I can't quite believe it myself. It is supposed to be the finest in the fleet! Only the very best get to serve aboard.

And here I am, a lowly cadet fresh from the Academy, and I'm to begin today. I have no idea why I was even picked. I've heard rumors that the Captain liked my conduct, or something similar. I can't believe it...oh wait I said that already.

The Captain! She is another legend in her own right. No ship under her command has ever missed a delivery, or gotten lost. Her direction is supposed to be beyond expert, and she has been with the fleet for longer than anyone can remember.

I don't really have any experience to speak of, besides some training flights in the Academy simulator. What could they possibly see in me?

I still can't quite believe what is happening.

I'm going to have to stop here if not I will be late. I must remind myself to write to Mother and the rest soon.

★★★★★★

Day 5

I've been introduced to everyone and have learned a bit about what my duties on the ship will be. I'm quite relieved to know that I won't have to do that much.

The crew has all been very nice to me. I think they may... take a bit of getting used to, but I'm sure we will get along fine. (I hope!)

I have not seen the Captain at all. Apparently she keeps to herself most of the time. It's a pity (I really want to meet her!) but I guess she must be very busy.

★★★★★★

Day 14

I have sort of gotten used to things aboard...I think. It is still rather hard to bring my emotions into the navigation. In the Academy we are taught the use of the traditional light-based flight systems, of course, but the anscryl is another thing entirely. It's good that I am only an assistant pilot and that the Captain herself will set the course and steer.

All I have to do is keep my emotions steady and focused into the system, just like they taught us at school. It is not exactly easy but not that hard either.

I spoke more with the First Mate today. He/she (is that how I should be writing it? his/her race has no definite gender, after all) was all business, but very professional. I had some questions about handling the apparatus which he/she answered quickly and accurately.

I don't know...I guess I still haven't gotten used to dealing with non-humans. I should have taken more classes on interspecies etiquette back at the Academy. I cannot tell what they are thinking most of the time, and I am afraid to give offense. I have not spoken to the Second Mate yet but I do hope that he will be friendlier.

★★★★★★

Day 15

I wrote to everyone today. I hope for a reply from them before we depart, but I don't think that is likely. Still, I don't really mind. I am busy enough as it is with the preparations and everything else that has to be done.

★★★★★★

Day 18

We're still at the preparatory stage. We have to get the supplies on board, calibrate the delivery mechanisms, things like that. It's a lot to do! It's only now that I appreciate everything that they put us through in class. It was difficult but thorough training.

I find myself a little worried about actually starting our voyage, but it is probably just preflight jitters. After all, I'm actually aboard the Melchissor, and I'm actually going to... alright, must calm myself down, getting excited won't help anyone or anything.

★★★★★★

Day 21

Takeoff! It's not a big a deal as it seems. Anscryl travel is unlike other forms of transport. One moment you're here and the next you're...not. Actually according to the classes at the Academy you actually are still here, but not in the way that conventional matter is "here" Rather you are "here" but at the same time "there" because – I don't understand it myself.It all flew way over my head when I first heard it, and even now when I'm actually in the midst of anscryl travel, it doesn't make any more sense.

Good thing being a pilot (or assistant pilot, rather) doesn't require you to know any of this! If it did I'm quite sure I would not be here.

I thought it would be much harder but so far things have been relatively easy. I don't even really need to concentrate that hard, just maintain my attention and endeavor not to become too startled or excited by anything. The crew is all extremely competent (they have to be! this is the Melchissor and...breathe, breathe, control yourself!) and I have yet to see any errors being made in any department – navigation, energy redirection, anything.

It actually looks like this might be easy!

★★★★★★

Day 29

I can't quite believe it, but things have gotten to be routine to some degree. We are still in the between space and have not made contact with any of the worlds yet, so all there is to do is perform maintenance, sit quietly, and wait.

It is kind of interesting being the only human on board. There were so many of us in the Academy, but here I am the only one. I do hope I have not offended them in any way. First Mate goes about his/her business as usual, Second Mate is sometimes here and sometimes not (that is how they are I think) and there are some others who I don't think I've even seen.

Maybe they don't exist on this plane, or are displaced during anscryl travel. I've heard that that is quite common actually.

Whatever the case the ship is on its way! I would say I can't wait, but actually we seem to do every day IS wait. And in waiting, we actually move forwards - I don't think I'll ever understand anscryl travel.

★★★★★★

Day 33

Our first delivery! It went off without a hitch, I'm glad to report. It was simple enough - keep the craft steady as it went in, focus on the controls, and that was that. Just like we learnt in school.

I was...happy afterwards. Very happy. It is such a joy to be able to give others what they need, and they definitely needed what we had to give. It felt good.

I look forwards to many other deliveries like this.

★★★★★★

Day 45

I have been thinking about my home planet more as the days go by. Our voyage is smooth and we have made many successful deliveries, but it is the ones that fail that weigh on me the most heavily. The Captain has been most kind and says that my sadness has not in any way affected navigation or astrogation, but maybe she is just being nice.

Still, it makes me wonder. My planet was one of the failures, you see. We did not - could not - accept what they brought at that time, and that doomed us. It was only after the land had been split and the mountains blown apart that they came again, and this time the whole world was so full of despair that it was almost as if everyone had no choice but to accept what had been offered.

My mother would always tell me that her prayers had been answered and that it was the gods themselves that sent down the ships. She is not clear on the specifics, but then again, how could she be? She didn't even know what it was that had come down from the skies to bring salvation. Neither did I. And now here I am, on one of those same ships. It's strange how things turn out.

I am fortunate beyond words to have been saved (even though I cannot remember it), and to have a chance to save others. Or at least try to. The last one we visited...I don't know. I just don't know.

Why? Why don't they see? Why do they refuse our gifts? They need them so badly, and yet they turn away...why? It makes me sad beyond words. I wanted to ask the other crewmembers about it but I don't want to sound rude.

Still, I find myself thinking about it all the time now. Sometimes I can't sleep. Why do they not wish to accept what they really need?

I...I can't continue, if not it really will affect my ability to assist with piloting.

★★★★★★

Day 49

I got a reply from everyone today! It's hard to receive messages in between flights, but somehow the First Mate managed it. I must be sure to thank him/her later.

Big Sister is so proud of me! It makes me blush just to think about it. I can see Mother going around to brag to all her friends. I wish she wouldn't but I know that she will do it anyway.

One of my uncles has just gotten married. I'm happy for him, but I also wish I could be there to attend the ceremony and congratulate the newlyweds. Duty calls, though. I feel so adult when I say that!

I know I should not have undue feelings of pride, (they may affect the navigation) but still I can't help but feel some. I shall try not to let them get the better of me.

I can't reply while in transit but I will think of them every day.

★★★★★★

Day 51

I thanked First Mate for his/her assistance in intercepting the messages from my family. I think I am getting more used to his/her mannerisms...when he/she turns away it does not mean he/she is displeased, that is just how he/she is.

★★★★★★

Day 53

Another day, another delivery. I don't think it will ever get to the point where I am used to how things work. The first few were easy, but the some of them...the star currents were hard to read coming in, let alone navigate while in the stream itself! I don't know how the Captain manages it. I guess there is a reason she is the Captain. It was all I could do to keep things as steady as possible.

I think I did a pretty good job, but I still feel worried whenever we come in for an approach, or during takeoff. So many things could go wrong...and yet, nothing does, because of the crew.

I'm part of all that too! I still can't really believe it. But I have been thanked more than once for my handling of the ship. First Mate came up to place a clawed hand on my shoulder and I was surprised and delighted at his/her words of praise. I haven't seen Second Mate around but I can feel his appreciation from the bulkhead where he is stationed.

It's such an honor, truly. I must continue to do my best in future.

★★★★★★

Day 55

I have spoken (is that the right word again? thought?) to the Second Mate about my feelings regarding the failed deliveries. I had assumed that making as many trips at they did that they would be less and less affected by each new one, but his reply surprised me. He pulsed (there, that's the right word, they are light-based entities after all) that he too felt sad, and that his feelings did not diminish. In fact, they sometimes grew stronger. Handling the sadness and pain when they refuse is also one of our duties, he told me.

But he was quick to also tell me that he loved the times when they did accept our gifts, when we made a difference and they were grateful. I told him I felt the same.

Somehow I worked up the courage to ask what the Captain herself thought. He pulsed a warm glow (I think they is how they smile) and pulsed that I would have to ask her myself.

I don't know if I can! I don't think I have spoken to her more than once before on this entire voyage. She has spoken to me a few times, yes, but those were mainly routine instructions and the like. I still get the shivers when I think that I am actually onboard with the Captain of the Melchessoir, even though it has been quite a while already!

I must remember to calm down. That gets easier day after day as well. Maybe I really am getting the hang of this.

★★★★★★

Day 67

We have completed the first leg of our journey. It seems like such a long time since I boarded the ship, but in another sense it feels just like yesterday. I guess travel by anscryl is like that – it messes up your perceptions even as it sharpens them.

I received my first reprimand today. To be honest I had been waiting for it. I know that my emotions are not as stable as they could be. Second Mate was very clear about what I was to do and what I was not. The deliveries to be handled with great control and I could not my wayward feelings compromise it in any way. I apologized.

Still, it is not something I can completely control, even with the Academy training. I realize now the truth of what my instructor always told me – do not close yourself off from what you feel, but rather merge with one, become it. Ride with it, so that it is not about you controlling it or it you, but whatever you are feeling and whatever you are being one and the same, yet distinct. It was hard to understand at that time but I think I see the truth of what he is saying now.

And what emotions there are! I am so happy when one of the worlds can accept what we are bringing. Even if they cannot see or perceive us, when they do accept the gift I am beside myself with joy.

I shall resolve to do better next time.

★★★★★

Day 71

Nothing much to report. I believe that I can say now that I have gotten used to the way things work here. My emotions are a lot more stable, and though the First and Second Mates do not say anything I think I can sense their pleasure (at least Second's glow has changed in a way that I think means happiness)

There is a lot more navigation to do than normal, so I will keep this entry short.

★★★★★

Day 77

More deliveries. Things are becoming almost routine. Keep it stable, come in for landing, align with the planet's rotation and then commence delivery. I've done it so many times now.

I think the most important thing that I've realized is to let the Captain handle it. She really knows what she is doing. I just have to do my part and let everyone else do theirs.

It feels good. Sometimes even better than a successful delivery. I know that I am part of something greater, something important, and I truly feel grateful to be aboard the ship.

★★★★★

Day 88

We are nearing our final destination. I have asked the crew why this was the last, and they replied that it was because it was a delicate case.

Their fates hang in the balance and First Mate says that they may very well destroy themselves even if they accept our gift. I was not saddened as much by it as I thought I would be. Perhaps I have grown up more on this journey than I thought.

All I can do - all we can do - is do our best. I have to keep telling myself that.

★★★★★★

Day 97

Today I spoke with the Captain.

It happened quite by accident. I was doing routine maintenance on the onboard systems when I heard a soft chime, and then she called my name.

I was so surprised that I almost dropped my scanner. I turned to face the main monitor and I saw the blinking lights that signaled that she was online. All around me the screens flickered blue, then green, then red and then blue again. She wanted to speak to me.

I didn't know what to say. I stood there in shock for moments, casting my eyes from one screen to another. What could I say? This was the Captain of a Melchissor, a legend in her own right, and she was talking to me personally! But before I could say anything, she spoke.

"You've been doing good work. Keep it up."

I mumbled a reply, something about how honored I was, but to be honest I was still in shock. She was talking to me...really talking to me. And it wasn't part of routine announcements or navigational instructions or anything like that.

Moments passed and I could tell she was waiting for me to say something. Somehow I worked up my courage enough to ask what I had always wanted to know.

"How do they see us? I know they can't really perceive us. Do they know we're here?" I hear the soft chime of her voice reply.

"Some would call us good, some evil. On some worlds we are known as angels, on other demons."

I had no idea what where these angels and demons she referred to, but what she said explained many things. Why some would reject the light, and some would cherish it. Why some could not even see us, and some would see us as something else entirely. There was only so much I could tell from the ship readouts, but what she said made sense.

We spent several moments there in silence. I looked out to the field of stars beyond the ship and I realized that there were uncountable worlds out there. This was the Melchissor, but there were many others in the fleet that travelled on wings of speed, light and time, ferrying precious cargo to those in need.

How would we ever reach them all? Maybe it was impossible, but we had to try our best.

I turned back to the blinking readouts. Another chime and her voice came through again. It was like she could tell what I was thinking - and knowing the Captain, maybe she could. "Do not worry. If even we do not manage to save them all, what we do is worthwhile. Always remember that."

I nodded. I had seen the good that our work has done. Even if some of our gifts were rejected, the ones that were not made all the difference, and for that I was grateful.

There was nothing else to be said, and for a time we simply stood on deck together, watching the stars.

★★★★★★

Day 100

We are here, the final planet on our journey. I am almost homesick but then I remember that the anscryl will bring me back to the day before our journey has even begun. The longer the journey, the earlier it returns you to...once again I don't pretend to understand how it works, only that it does.

I must confess to some degree of trepidation. Even though the Captain manages the approach (as she does in every case) with finesse and skill, I still need to maintain enough emotional stability for her to bring the ship in properly. I keep repeating to myself what I have been taught. "Ride, don't force" and it seems to work. I've done this many times since I first came on board, but this trip is different. The currents are fiercer, and I have to use every inch of self-control to keep my emotions in check.

All this goes out the window, though, when I see it. The ship rocks back and forth and First Mate scowls at me from the side but I am too awestruck to notice.

It is beautiful.

The Melchissor sways slightly again and our timescale shifts with it, but I am too awed to even apologize.

It is a brilliant shade of blue and green, the clouds swirling atop its surface forming a patina of white. There is none of the unbroken grey that so characterizes the other planets that we have been to. There have been wars, yes, but none that have cracked the surface of the land and evaporated the seas. It's still unspoiled, still pristine, still beautiful.

I know we are not supposed to speak, or even to think, during approach and disengagement, but my discipline that has served me so well on so many previous journeys cracks. I cannot control myself and I blurt out the words.

"Will they accept it? They have to, right? It would be...it would be the worst thing ever if they didn't." I start shaking from emotion, and I have to breathe deeply to even calm down a bit.

Second Mate guides me back to my seat gently with his warm glow even as the First lays his/her hand on my shoulder. I get the impression that this is not the first time they have seen this reaction.

"We cannot know." The Captain's voice is as gentle as always. "We have been here many times. Each time, they grow, but each time, they also forget."

"We will come as many times as we must. As long as some of them call out to us, there is still hope. I hope, too, that they will save themselves."

"How many times have we come? How many?" All sense of equanimity has long since slipped away from me. The planet is too beautiful, and the cries of its people are too painful to listen to any longer. I want to know. I MUST know.

"We are not the first ship that has come this way, nor will we be the last." The Captain replies.

"They are a...unique case. Sometimes our gift gets through, sometimes not. Sometimes only half of it is brought home. Sometimes none. We can never tell."

"How many more times will we come back?"

"As many as it takes. When they are ready, they will save themselves. And then we will be there to help them." The Captain's voice, always strong and steady, now has a note of something I have never heard before. Compassion? No...that is always there. It is resolve. Unending, unyielding resolve. To come back and give what is needed, as many times as it takes.

I close my eyes. As many times as it takes...how many more? I've of late learned to hear through the instruments what the people of the planet are saying. So many cry out for release, but so many more shut out everything that they do not wish to hear. Such hatred, such pain...I do not know how Second Mate can stand it, since they are far more attuned to emotion than us humans.

I open my eyes to see everyone already bent to their tasks. We cannot stay any longer. Home calls, and then rest, and then many more deliveries must be made, to planets besides this one. To everyone who needs what we have to give. To all who cry out for hope.

But even so...I cannot tear my eyes away from that verdant green and lustrous blue. The snowy clouds which swirl in patterns across its surface. The people that fight among themselves even as they scream for deliverance.

I don't even know its name – we are not allowed to know any of their names, lest we become too attached – but I know that it will stay in my memory forever. And I know too that I will be back, aboard this ship of light, to give hope to as many that call out for it.

As many times as it takes. Until their hearts are open enough to ask for and receive what they truly need.

I have never been as devout as my mother is, but as the Melchissor turns and leaves I find myself mouthing a silent prayer to whoever may be listening. May they learn what they truly need to, and be open to us the next time we come. And may I be there to watch them if they do.

The Station at the Edge

YOU SEE ALL sorts, out here. You really do.

I haven't been stationmaster all that long, actually, and here I am talking like I've seen it all. Nothing could be farther from the truth. I only got this post what like...3 years ago? If I recall correctly. And I don't think that I do. When you get to my age your memory starts playing tricks on you and you can't really tell this from that or what from what anymore.

But 3 years...that's long enough to know that you find all sorts out here.

It's the trains, you see. They don't go from one place to one place, or one time to one time. I mean, they do, but not all regular and linear-like. They crisscross each other, and go up and down in all sorts of crazy ways. Don't ask me how it all happens, I'm just the stationmaster.

What do you mean, I should know? I don't run the damn place. It runs itself, more like. I just issue the tickets and give out the tickets and that's it. That's it.

There has to be someone at the other side, y'know, to receive the people in the trains and tell them where to go and all that. Or maybe they just get out and they know where it is they're going. I don't even know why there has to be a stationmaster in the first place. Everything's all automated these days...why there can't be machines or flashing lights or something so an old man can go home and get some rest, huh? Like I said I don't run the place, I just give out the tickets.

Who comes here? All sorts, like I said. Why, just the other day the cutest girl you ever did see was just –

What? I'm a lech? I shouldn't be checking out the girls while I'm on the job? I'll have you know that I was happily married for 20 years. Whatever happened later? None of your goddamn business.

So she was sitting there, waiting for the train. She was serious, though, I'll tell you that. Her eyes were somber, almost fierce. She was wearing one of those schoolgirl outfits...looked weird, it did. 'Specially because she was carrying a sword.

What? Are you deaf or something? Yeah, you heard me right. She was carrying a sword, one of those fancy-ass Japanese things. Katanas, I think they call 'em. It was all wrapped up nice and proper like and she had it in front of her while she sat on the station bench. Could have made a pretty postcard, she could.

Sometimes they don't like to talk, so I just waited there with her. She was one of the non-talking ones. She didn't seem the company and neither did I, so after I sold her the ticket I just sat ther...don't start that, when I said I just sat there that's all I did.

"Where do the trains go?" she asked suddenly.

I told her what I told you, that I didn't rightly know, that they came from someplace and they left for someplace. She stood up for a while and walked to the edge of the tracks, looking outwards. Then she nodded, seemed to come to some kind of decision. She walked back to me and asked another question.

"The next train...do you know where it goes?" I told her I didn't and she seemed ok with that.

Her hand tightened around the bundle she was carrying. The katana thingy. She bowed and fixed me with that stare of hers one more time, strong and powerful enough to pierce metal, it felt like. Then as the next train pulled up, she stepped onto it and was gone.

I don't know who she was or where she was going. You never can tell with these folk.

That was just the first one. She stands out in my mind for some reason, must have been her looks. Or her eyes. Or that bundle she was carrying. I don't rightly know myself.

Since then they've been many more. Fifty? A hundred? I lose count. Yeah, don't think you're so special, you're just one of the crowd.

You're not here to take a train? Well you coulda fooled me. Then why didn't you say so in the first place? Quit bothering me and get back to...

You want to listen? Sure, suit yourself. I'm just an old guy who sits around here doing nothing. Nothing except tell stories and give out tickets that is.

You want another one...well, there was this robot from a while ago. How do I know it was a robot? Don't be an idiot. It had those thingums and whatsists and stuff flashing around all over, what else was it going to be?

So the robot comes up to me and asks me, all polite as can be, where the trains are going. What, do I look like some sort of travel agent? Am I like a directory or something? They all want to know the same thing and I always give the same answer. I don't know. I just give out tickets is all.

First the girl, then a robot. What's next, a talking plant? Anyway, the robot just stares at me with all its lights blinking and for a moment I think it's gonna hurt me or something...you can't tell with robots, they don't exactly have a face you can read easily. So I stare right back.

Then suddenly it rights itself and it goes off back the way it came. Doesn't even take a ticket. Strange eh?

Like I said, you get all sorts out there.

★★★★★★

Oh, so you're back again. Hi there.

What, you think just because I said hello to you we're friends now? You got another thing coming if you think that way! I don't make friends with just anybody. No sirree. You get to my age, you have standards. And you don't qualify, not by a long shot.

Now you're going to want another story. How do I know? I just know. You don't spend all this time here without figuring some things out. It's the way you sit there, all fidgety and stuff. You keep on looking down and then keep on looking up at me. That tells me you want more stories, loud and clear.

So I told you about the girl, and the robot. What's next? Lemme think about it for a second.

Yeah...yeah, it's coming to me. There was this guy, see. I know, I know, there's tons of guys. But this guy was different.

He had a trenchcoat on, and a fedora. Looked like he was in a spy movie or something. You know, those spy movies were the best. I loved them when I was a kid. You always knew who the good guys were in those. They were the ones with the brown coats and the guns and, yeah everyone had guns, but the bad guys had black coats and they...alright, alright, I'll get on with it.

So yeah, the guy comes and looks at me all serious-like and says "Where did she go?"

I ask "Who?"

He says "the girl with the sword. Where did she go?"

Now I'm not sure I like the look of this guy, so I don't respond right away. I sort of look left and look right and I give him the ol' squinty eye and then I shake my head again.

"I don't know."

He just stares at me, a cold gimlet-eyed look that makes me think that he may not be one of the good guys after all. In any case his coat was grey, so I couldn't tell.

He doesn't say a word and boards the next train. I don't know whether or not I should hope that he finds the girl or not. Whatever. It doesn't concern me anyway.

★★★★★★

You. You again. Can't you leave an old man in peace? Why do you have to keep on asking me your stupid questions?

You're going to want to know about someone else this time, right?

Ahhh...I get it. You think there's some kind of pattern here right? Like the robot is the girl's guardian or something, and he's protecting her from the spy movie guy, and

No, no it doesn't work that way. It's all random out here. People, things, machines...they just come and go. There's no reason for it.

Why are you looking at me like that for? You don't believe me? Well, go see for yourself. When you've been sitting here as long as I have, you - hey, waitaminute! Where are you going? What do you think you're doing?

You're leaving? Bah, go ahead. See if I care.

★★★★★★

So, you're back again. What happened to you leaving? Couldn't leave an old man in peace huh?

Yeah, I know. I know that look. You want more stories. Demanding, aren't you?

No, I've got no more to tell. Not to the likes of you! Leaving an old man here to...whaddaya mean you weren't leaving me alone? Just needed to go somewhere for a while? A likely story.

Why are you looking at me like that? Now you're going to say that I remind you of someone. Well, I don't rightly care if I do or I don't.

What? You say the guy I was talking about sounds familiar? The one with the hat? That he reminds of someone? Who? You haven't even been here a quarter as long as I have. What do you know? Nothing, that's what. Don't think you can be telling me anything now, d'ya hear!

★★★★★★

Haven't seen you for some time.

You know, the way you're looking at me seems kind of familiar. I think I've seen it somewhere before...can't quite place it though.

Stop staring. It's rude. Don't they teach you that where you come from? No? Well, then you haven't been brought up properly.

What do I remember? Why do you care? And if I tell you you're just going to keep asking more questions. I know your game - you just want to bug an old man to death, that's what you want to do.

Humor you? I guess I could. It's not like I have anything better to do anyway.

I remember...I remember I was looking for something. I'm not sure what it was. I think I came here to find it. But then I got stuck here selling tickets somehow and...no, no I just can't place it. Bah.

You! Now you're gotten me thinking and I can't get it out of my mind. I won't be able to get it out of my mind and I'll here be thinking about it for God knows how long. It's all your fault too...I hope you're satisfied with yourself!

Don't give me that "I didn't mean it" bullcrap. You totally meant it and I know it. You want to know...you've wanted to know for as long as you first laid eyes on me! You've just been waiting till it's the right time is all. Yeah, yeah, I know what you

Go on, get out of here! Leave an old man to think in peace. After all, you started it, you could have at least the decency to leave me alone now.

★★★★★★

I've been thinking. I've been thinking a whole lot.

It's you, you know? You're the one who's got me thinking like this. All that old stuff, who I am, why I ever came here in the first place. Now it's got me between the ears and it won't let me go.

I wonder...I really wonder, you know? I can't actually remember what I did before I came here. I was a...no, no, can't remember a thing. Total blank. Nothing. It's driving me nuts, that's what it's doing.

Why'd you have to go and do that? Get me thinking and all. Here I was, just minding my own business, and you have to come up and ask me dumb questions. Like about who came here before, and what there is to do, and all that kind of stuff. Especially about where I came from.

Don't just sit staring! Go on, get out of here. Leave an old man alone to think. It's all your fault anyway, you started it.

★★★★★★

The trains...they've started looking different, they have. They move slower, and they look more solid. Like I should, I don't know, see where they're going. Even though I know I can't see where they are going.

Why're you looking at me that way? I forgot...you always look at me like that. Like I got two heads or something.

Sit down. Yeah, I mean it. Sit down here next to me. You must get pretty tired standing all the time. Not to mention asking me stupid questions. Stop jabbering and just keep an old man company for a while.

190

I forgot to ask...what's going on with you? Why are you here? What's this all mean to...oh no, now, don't give me that, shaking your head and all. You get to ask me questions but I don't get to ask you any? That's hardly fair.

Never mind. Let's just both shut up and watch the trains for a while.

★★★★★★

I think it's time for me to go. Yeah, I'm pretty sure of it now. It's the trains...they're calling to me. Like I have to jump on the next one that comes. I probably will, come to think of it.

Maybe I'll get to figure out what's the problem with that robot and the girl. I kind of really want to know what happened to her. No, get your mind out of the gutter. It's not just that she's pretty. I just kind of care for her, you know? Like an uncle or something. I hope she's ok.

Don't know about the others. There's plenty more I never told you about. This farmer with a bag of seeds, real worried he was. Not sure where he was bound for but he sure seemed in a hurry to get there. A fisherman with this harpoon thingy. A guy on a bike. A fairy princess - not as pretty as the girl, but with the brightest wings you ever did see. You see all sorts, out here. They all sort of blur together after a while.

Now you got me reminiscing about my time here. That's all you're good for, isn't it? Asking an old man stupid questions.

Ah, don't be like that. You know I'm just joking, right?

I don't think I ever noticed how nice this place really is. I mean, you got the trains, for once. Those are always nice to watch. But these benches look great too. All solid and brown and sturdy...they're made of, whatcha call it, oak? Yeah. And the tracks are this coal black, deep and dark and just...just great, you know?

The air, too, there's something about it. The way the light catches it and it throws up a kind of...dust? Then in falls down slowly and it just looks so pretty, especially when the trains come in.

Argh, I'm not good with words. I don't know half of what I'm saying. It's just a good place, that's what it is.

I'm going to miss it all, I think.

★★★★★★

I know what you are. You're my replacement, right? Yeah, you can't fool me. I've been around too long for that to work.

I know you have it. C'mon, stop making an old man wait around. It's there, isn't it? Out with it, now.

There we go.

You know, I've never really looked at one of these closely before. It does look nice now, doesn't it? Kind of like a silvery-gold color. It sort of flickers when you look at it real close.

Alrighty then. Time for me to board the train. I think one's coming soon. What do you mean there's no sound? Huh, you stay here for as long as I did and you don't need sound to tell when one's coming in. You just know.

You take care, y'hear? You go on and take care of yourself. Don't wait for me. Just do what you're here to do.

Don't look at me like that. Giving out tickets ain't that bad of a job...I should know, I've been doing it for the longest time now. It'll be fine, trust me. You'll get used to it in no time.

Who's gonna keep you company? You keep yourself company, that's what. I was here for God knows how long and all I had was myself to talk to. That's how I ended up like this... no, they'll be more trains, you'll see. You're gonna have plenty of company.

Are you crying? You can't be crying now. We barely know each other. What the...there, there. It's gonna be fine. You'll see.

Okay. I really have to go now. They're waiting for all, you see. The girl and the robot and that guy and all the others

I've never told you about before. I'm sure they'll all out there, somewhere.

Best of luck, sonny. Whatever the case it's not going to be boring. You see all sorts, out here.

But then, you already know that, don't you?

To the End of the World

OUT HERE, PEOPLE always ask me where I'm going. The same question each time, and I always give the same answer.

"I'm going to the end of the world."

I get a lot of looks. I get more than that too. I get people laughing at me, snorting, shaking their heads. People tell me to go back, to where I came from (like they know where I came from?) They don't believe me, that much I can tell. I don't quite believe myself most of the time either.

But in the end it doesn't change anything. I've been going there for a long time and I'm not about to stop now. So I just smile - not sense in making anyone angry - and I get back on my bike and I keep on going.

★★★★★★

Things look different out here too. The lights, the trees, the roads...they all look kind of weird, kind of funny. They're all kind of grey, and misty, and they sometimes look like a light is shining through them. It looks kind of cool but it also looks scary at the same time.

Part of it might be how I'm travelling. I don't exactly use the normal roads. It's this bike, see - not your everyday run-of-the-mill one, that's for sure. When I get on and start riding everything starts looking strange. I get a lot farther than I can recall travelling, and sometimes I can't even remember when and where I started the journey. It doesn't really bother me as long as we get to where I'm going.

Speaking of not being able to remember...I'm not sure how and where I got it. It's always been with me for as long as I can remember. I've been on the road for a long, long time, and I can't recall a time when I didn't have the bike with me.

This bike and me - we go way back...way, way, WAY back, even. I've always thought of giving it a name but I can't think of one. I feel I should - I mean, we've been together so long that I feel it's like my brother or something! - but I can never find one that sticks. So I just call it my bike. I think it likes that even more than a name.

So we keep on travelling, and we keep on getting further to where we've gotta go to. How do I know? I don't, but my bike does, and that's good enough for me. Yeah, I can always trust it to keep me on the straight and narrow, and avoid all those nasty potholes and dirt tracks that are hell on my tires.

We keep going, that's what we do. Keep going until we get to the end of the world.

★★★★★★

I have to stop over at quite a few places on the road. You know, supplies and all that. My bike doesn't need refueling. Yeah, I told you, it's not like the others. But me, I gotta eat. I don't care for nothing fancy, but if I don't eat then I die and if I die I'm not going anywhere. And the tires need some looking at now and then.

I don't much like to talk but I like to listen, and people on the road have a lot of stories to tell. I hang out where they are all gather together, the truckers and the gangers and the bikers (the ones besides me, that is) The ones with the strange hair and the others with spikes in their bodies. Some are short and hunched over, some are thin, tall and gangly, and others still are muscled and tough.

They talk about all sorts of things, from huge moths that they swore flew into their windscreens - and they meant HUGE, like 5 meters across! - to tall, dark strangers who chased them from one town to the next. Rainbows that were all black and grey, shining down from beyond the horizon. Flickering lights that took the shape of trees, and whirlwinds of dust which spoke to them.

It's all very interesting but in the end I have to get back to where I'm going. So I wave goodbye to the others and I plunk my behind on the seat and I'm off once more.

★★★★★★

I take a turning somewhere - I don't really know where, you can't tell with these things - and there she is. A girl.

I blink and I shake my head and I blink again. I must be seeing things. There's never anything on the roads that I take - nothing except me, generally. Just trees and rocks and sand... no people. Like I said, I don't use normal roads. All the other bikes, the cars, the hover-jets and what have you - I never see them. Ever.

But yet she's there, in a little pink dress (pretty cute, I must say) and she has one hand out, thumb up. A hitchhiker.

I stop the bike to get a better look and she just looks at me.

She's a cute one, and it's not just the dress. I haven't seen a girl in a long time, but I'm not one of those guys who just jumps at any pretty face they see, no sirree. I try to be a gentleman if I do say so myself. My road is a long one, and a strange one, and it just ain't right to be asking a girl to share it, 'specially as I don't know where it'll take me.

But this girl - she just keeps on looking at me with the most serious expression that you could ever imagine. It scares me a little.

"Looking for a ride?" I say. It's a stupid question and I know it. I mean, she has her hand and thumb out and everything. It should be obvious what she wants.

"Yes." she replies, clear as day.

I don't know what to say next. I sort of kick my heels around a bit and hem and haw. I look down and then up and then sideways and then back and she's still looking at me.

"Ummmm, you know it's kind of dangerous out here. Especially for a young girl like you." Her eyes say that she doesn't give a damn. I don't even need to ask.

I look at her for a few seconds more. She looks back. It doesn't look like she'll take no for an answer. I sigh.

"Well, come on up. There's enough space on this thing for two." She does, and I put my foot on the pedals, and we both hit the road again.

★★★★★★

So somehow I end up with a young girl riding pillion. I must admit, it feels real pleasant to have something soft and smooth press up against your back like that while you're riding. I mean, it's not like I have the hots for her or anything like that. I like the feel of the wind on my face, and my hands on the handlebars, and the thrumming of the engine beneath me. But she feels a different kind of good. Nice.

She's a quiet one, too. Hasn't said anything for the past day or so. Just sits there all silent-like, hands on my shoulders. If not for her constant warmth I could forget that she's even there most of the time.

We pass by cities and lakes and torn-down buildings. I always feel kind of sad when I see the buildings. They feel so... lonely. People must have lived there at some time, but now they're all gone, leaving them empty and abandoned. I don't much like thinking of those things, so I take my eyes away and look at something else - which just happens to be the road. Which keeps going on and on.

I can't ignore the fact that the girl is on my back, so I try to strike up a conversation now and then, ask her where she's from and all that, but she doesn't so much as say a word. Eventually I give up asking and just keep riding.

★★★★★★

You see a lot of strange stuff on the road, and not just what the folks at the watering holes keep on talking about. I guess you could call them ghosts? I've never pegged myself as the superstitious type, but I have no idea what to call them.

They come up towards us as we ride on, all grey and misty-like. Some take the shape of trees and some birds but the ones that I get the most freaked out by are those that look like humans. They writhe and twist and reach out towards me. I gun the engine and make sure to stay way ahead of them. I don't know what they want but I get the feeling that I don't want to find out.

"They're crying." she says suddenly.

"Whassat? Huh?" I say, craning my neck around to see. I certainly don't see any tears coming out from them.

"Those things. They're crying." she says with utter certainty.

"How do you know that?"

She grows quiet again and I decide not to push it. Everyone's got their secrets.

We get a lot farther ahead from the ghosts (at least I'm sure that's what they are!) and I feel a sense of relief. Then I wonder why I've never seen any of this stuff before. Maybe it's the girl? Could be. My bike keeps me off the normal roads but this is strange even for me.

Doesn't do anything good to keep on thinking in this vein. Could just be another sighting or something like that. After all, it's not the first time I've seen something like this and I doubt it'll be the last.

★★★★★★

We're getting closer now, I can feel it. The scenery looks different - less trees and more arid land. The clouds are thinner and the light is brighter.

There isn't exactly a map to where I'm going. I just kind of... figure it out as I go along. My bike sort of knows, I think. I'm the rider but you gotta know when to let it take the lead. So I just put my foot on the pedal and I let the machine direct me.

She doesn't eat much. I give her some of my food and she just picks at it. I ask her if she doesn't like the taste and she looks at me and shakes her head no. At least she's polite.

So I ask her. "Why are you going to the end of the world anyway?"

She looks back at me. "Why are you?"

"Well...because I gotta. I don't know why myself." I think she should really ask my bike, not me, but I don't want her to think she's crazy. I don't think my bike would tell her anyway.

She doesn't reply and goes back to eating. I think I've gotten used to how quiet she really is.

I don't ask her any more questions and she doesn't either. After a while we get back on the bike and keep moving along.

★★★★★★

She makes me think, this girl. She does. I don't think I've ever asked myself why I'm going to the end of the world. It just seemed the thing to do.

It might have had to do with where I came from. It wasn't a good place, and being on the road for as long I've been, I can be more than sure about that.

It was after the war, see. There wasn't much of enough for anyone. The fields had been burnt up and the rivers had gone dry and well...even when we managed to scavenge enough to survive, that didn't mean we were happy. Far from it. The droids still wandered here and there and we had to be really careful not to get near to them if not we'd be dead. It was a lot of hiding, a lot of running, and not so much eating. And it went on for as long as I remember.

I guess one day I just got tired of things. I got tired of having to eke out a miserable existence that might end suddenly if I so much as stepped the wrong way into the path of a droid. So one day I just upped and left.

I can't remember if that was when I found the bike. Or it found me. Things were all in the daze that day...I had gotten out of the village and just keep on walking in one direction. I didn't know north from south, or east from west. I just knew that I wanted to be somewhere else - anywhere else. So I fumbled and stumbled and yeah, one day I found myself riding and I haven't looked back since.

It's funny how things work out. When I left all I could think to myself was just how much I wanted to get out of there. And then I found the bike somehow, and I went here and there and one day I decided to go to the end of the world. And then I pick up this girl and here I am.

★★★★★★

We still need food, and supplies, and so we stop. I warn her not to go off alone but she just ignores me and waltzes off into a nearby store. I have no idea what she's going to do there - I don't even think she has any money to buy anything with! But a week or so with her I know better than to ask.

I don't know why I let her travel with me. I'm not exactly lonely - I've got my bike, after all. It can't be for conversation - she doesn't even talk much. Maybe I just took pity on her that day when I saw her. Maybe not.

I guess it's the rules of the road...she put her thumb out and I had to answer. It's not like I don't have the extra space, after all. It can't hurt to have one more person with you now can it?

I sit around a while and whistle and tap my fingers on my handlebars. I go off to get some of my own supplies, but this time I don't bother to listen to the any of the gossip around the fires. Wouldn't do to keep the little lady waiting.

After a while she comes back and sits right on the back of the bike without saying anything at all. Typical. I sigh and I get in front. Time to hit the road again.

★★★★★★

There's a city in the distance now. I've never seen it before. Maybe we are going the right way after all.

I've tried asking her about where she comes from, what she's going to do, why she's here, but she just keeps quiet. She's interested in the city, though. Keeps on looking at it with those big eyes of hers. I would, too, if I didn't have to keep my eyes on the road. The terrain has gotten rougher here - potholes, cracks, stuff you really have to watch out for. My bike is good but it needs me to take care of it as much as it takes care of me.

The city...maybe that's really what lies at the end of the world. I always thought it was going to be a wall, or something like that. I mean, I didn't really except a sign or fireworks. Fireworks - those would be nice. Like they were gonna throw a party and only those that got there would be invited. That would be great.

I feel kind of excited about getting there now actually. Maybe there WILL be a party. I don't know what might be there and that makes me want to get there all the more. There's the city, but what's in it? Maybe there's something inside, or beyond. Sure, it could be dangerous, but we didn't come all this way to stop. I wanted to get to the end of the world, and now that we're almost there...I can't wait to get there.

We ride on for days and the damn thing doesn't get any closer. The girl doesn't look worried in the least - keeps right on looking at it every chance she gets, even when she's eating - but I'm getting a little antsy myself. I mean, I'm the one who's riding the bike and I gotta keep my eyes on the road and if it gets worse we might get thrown off and that would be the end of the road for us.

But things get better. The roads start to clear and bit by bit, slowly but surely, the city starts coming into view. It's the lights that reach us first - long and pale, then as we get closer the buildings become clearer. The stand out like silent sentinels in the night, tall and black. As we approach I can even make out windows, and then details on the buildings, and then -

I just keep on riding. We're gonna be there soon, so all I have to do is get there. There's no point in staring at it like she does when we're going to be there in less than a day.

★★★★★★

The gates are locked.

I guess I should have expected this. I mean, I go all this way and I finally get to the end of the world and the goddamn gates are locked. It's enough to make a grown man cry. Except that I don't cry easily, so I just kick the door and all I get is some pain in my foot for all my trouble.

While I'm jumping around looking like an idiot, the girl just walks up to the door, puts her hand on it, and then turns to me.

"You need to put your hand on the door."

What? I need to put my hand on the door? How does she know that? I think about asking her but we all know how well that works. So after the pain dies down and I can walk normally again I do as she says.

The doors slide open, and while I'm standing there with my mouth open, the girl just walks in.

The inside of the place is big. Like, really big. Huge, even. It's massive. It's bigger than anything I've ever seen before, and I've seen a lot of things. Mountains taller than whole cities. Seas and valleys so wide it would take my bike months to get through them. But this place seems bigger than all of them.

I can't keep my mouth shut but the girl waltzes in like she's been here before. Maybe she has. How do I know?

It's just so...so...big. I know I've said it before but I don't really know how else to talk about it. I follow her slowly, looking around every which way. There are pillars that stretch to the ceiling, so tall I can't see where they end. The floor has been polished to a sheen so I can see my reflection in it. Our footsteps echo through the wide open space,

It looks like some kind of...temple. Do they even have gods here, at the end of the world? Who built this place anyway? What about the other buildings? I'm sure I saw more than one. How come the inside looks bigger than the outside? More questions, and it doesn't look like I'm going to get any answers.

The girl keeps on walking onwards while I'm doing my whole confused tourist bit, so I hurry up and follow her before I lose her in this...city, building, temple thing. I guess I'm not going to get my party after all.

★★★★★★

She seems to know where she's going, so all I do is follow her.

We pass by a whole lot of places. Fountains with sculptures of strange water creatures leaping out and into them – not as big as the halls, but pretty damn big all the same. Long hallways with nothing in them. A planetarium with spinning globes and crescent moons and stars on the ceiling – so many, many stars. Galleries with pictures of places I've never seen before, even on all my travels on the bike.

While we're making our way through one of the halls she suddenly turns to me and for the first time I see an expression on her face. She looks...sad. I'm not sure why. I look back at her curiously and I'm about to ask something before she turns back as quickly as she turned around and runs off. For a small girl she can move really fast, and I have to struggle to keep up with her. There's no room for questions when you're out of breath, so she runs and I run and after a while we end up in another room.

Which is big – almost as big as the entrance hall. It's completely empty except for a dais of some kind in the middle and she goes up to it without a single word. Come to think of it, she hasn't said a word since she first saw the city. That's normal for her, but you'd expect more of a reaction when she got to where she'd been wanting to go to. This is the end of the world, after all.

I try to follow her up but she's faster than me, as usual. She steps onto the dais and a huge pillar of light springs up around her. It gets bigger and bigger, washing over me and the rest of the hall, and when it hits me something despite my best efforts I can't move a muscle. All I can do is look at her and see her staring back at me as she silently mouths something. Figures... we get all the way here and she finally decides to talk and I can't hear a thing she's saying.

The light gets so bright that I have to shield my face from the glare and when I finally look up she's gone. Just like that. I can move again and so I rush up to the dais but nothing happens. I even jump up and down and wave my arms around a few times for good measure but...nothing. Whatever it was that worked for her doesn't work for me, that's for sure.

I think about exploring some more but this place is so damn huge that I'm afraid I'll get lost. I can barely remember my way back to my bike, and I'm only sure about that because we walked in a straight line to get here.

This is a joke and a half. I get to the end of the world and I'm afraid to go deeper in. Not only was there no party, I've got nothing to show for it at all.

I turn around and cast one last glance back at the empty dais. Where did she go? Where did she even come from? Whatever. It all doesn't matter now anyway. Then I begin the long walk back to the entrance.

★★★★★★

So what was I? Some kind of delivery man? I was supposed to meet her and bring her there and do...what exactly? Send her away?

I don't rightly know myself, but all I have now is this bike of mine, and we are going to go home and sleep this thing off.

Except that I don't know where home is myself, now. All I had in my mind was to get to the end of the world, and now that we got there...I don't know what comes next. I'm not going back to the village, that's for sure. So where else do I go? I have no idea.

I guess my bike knows, though. Maybe it brought me to the girl in the first place. Maybe the girl brought the bike to me...naaah, can't be. But you never can tell with these things.

I walk back and knock the kickstand back, step on the accelerator and get all comfy in the front seat. At least with this bike you always know where you are. Get some fuel in, start the engine and you're off. No need for questions or answers when you're on the open road. It's just the wind at your back and your path in front of you.

Well, wherever it is that I'm going, I'm better get a move on fast. No sense in wasting time. There are places to see and things to do and roads to be travelled.

It's time to hit the road again.